# LOCKE

## Corps Security, Book 6

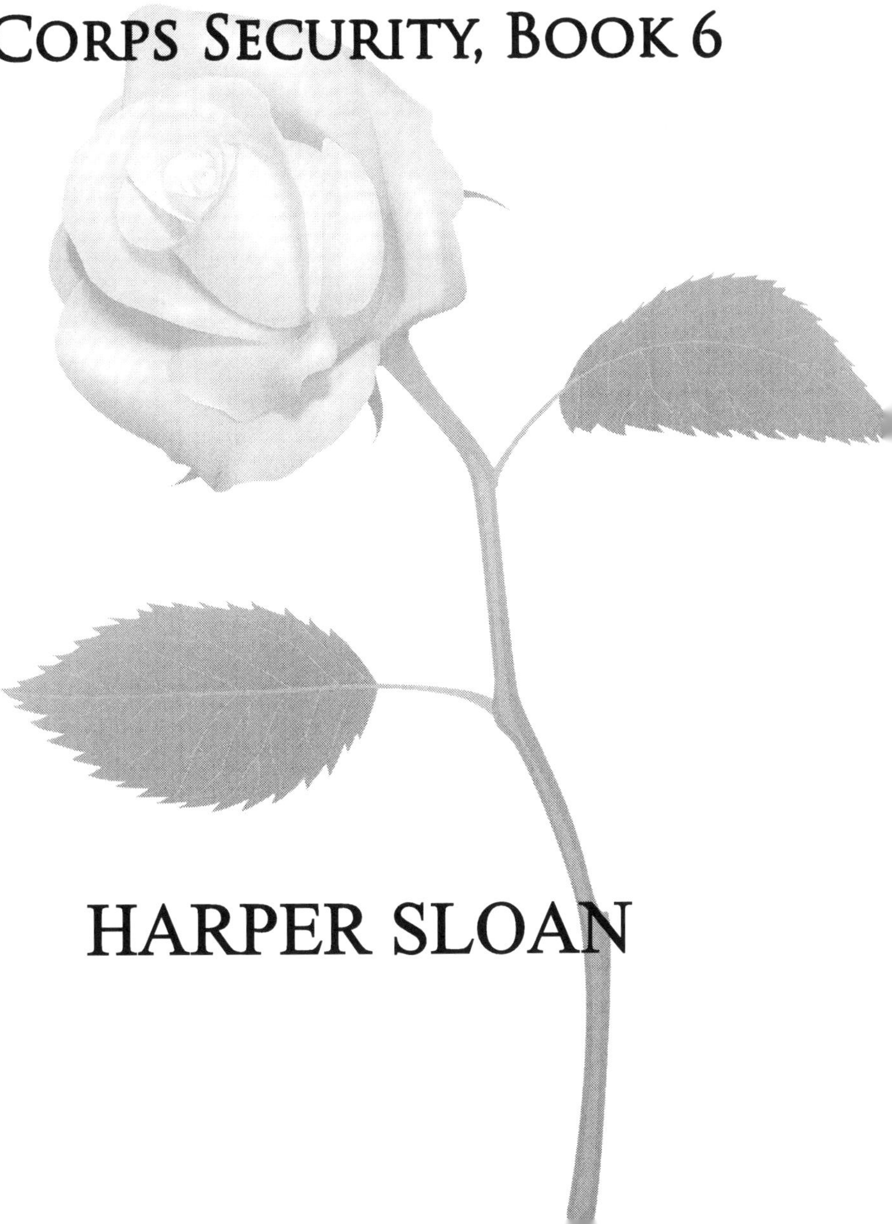

HARPER SLOAN

*Locke*

Copyright © 2014 by E.S. Harper

All rights reserved.

No part of this book may be reproduced or transmitted in any form or by any means, electronic or mechanical, including photocopying, recording, or by any information storage and retrieval system without the written permission of the author, except for the use of brief quotations in a book review.

This book is a work of fiction. Names, characters, places, and incidents either are the products of the author's imagination or are used fictitiously. Any resemblance to actual persons, living or dead, events, or locations is entirely coincidental.

All rights reserved. Except as permitted under the U.S. Copyright Act of 1976, no part of this publication may be reproduced, distributed, or transmitted in any form or by any means, or stored in a database or retrieval system, without the prior express, written consent of the author.

This book is intended for mature adults only.

Cover Design by Sommer Stein with Perfect Pear Creative Covers

Cover Photography by Michael Stokes

Editing by Mickey Reed

Paperback Formatting by Champagne Formats

ISBN 10: 1502400480

ISBN 13: 978-1502400482

# LOCKE PLAYLIST

Stupid Boy – preformed by Cassadee Pope

Demons – Imagine Dragons

Better Than Me – Hinder

Unconditionally – Katy Perry

This is What it Feels Like – Armin van Buuren

Wings – Birdy

Let Her Go – Passenger

Wasting All These Tears – Cassadee Pope

Back From the Dead – Skylar Grey

Run – Matt Nathanson feat. Sugarland

Searchlight – Phillip Phillips

I'll Follow You – Jon McLaughlin

Give Me Love – Ed Sheeran

Get Her Back – Robin Thicke

Shattered – Trading Yesterday

Watch Me – Paul McDonald & Nikki Reed

Stay With Me – Sam Smith

Chandelier – Sia

Human – Christina Perri

I Won't Give Up – Jason Mraz

Find You – Zedd

Build Me Up Buttercup – Gary Lewis & The Playboys

# DEDICATION

To my husband.
I kinda like you.
A lot.
Even when you snore.

To Contact Harper:

Email: Authorharpersloan@gmail.com
Website: www.authorharpersloan.com
Facebook: www.facebook.com/harpersloanbooks

Other Books by Harper Sloan:

AXEL

CAGE

BECK

UNCAGED

COOPER

Disclaimer:

This book is not suitable for younger readers. There is strong language, adult situations, and some violence.

# PROLOGUE
## *Maddox*

SIX WEEKS. It's been over a goddamn month since Emmy ran from me.

Just gone.

It took me three days to find her—thanks to the tracking device I had placed on her car—down in some small Podunk town in south Florida. Even if she had been trying to hide, she'd done a shit job of it. One search for her parents would have brought me right to her.

It took me longer to actually get eyes on her than it had to find her. She was holed up in some cheap-ass hotel for three weeks. She called in her meals and never left the room. And unfortunately, I had to leave and rush home when things out of my control needed attention and I again had to pull Asher's head out of his ass. Now I'm back and I'm not leaving until I get my hands on her.

She doesn't want to be found. I know that, but damn if I'm going to let her run off and get away for good. I've pushed and pushed her away. Every bone in my body has screamed at me to take what she's been offering for years. I've seen her, I know what she wants, but I won't let my demons hurt her. Not my Emmy.

Since day one, she's been the greatest temptation, but I refused to take everything innocent that is Emmy and let my blackness take her. Because that's what will happen. It will wrap around her soul and slowly choke the life out of her. Just like every other person I've allowed in.

I'll taint her. I'll ruin her. And in the end, it will destroy her.

One smile from her made me fall. So I pushed her away. I told her that she would never be what I need—that I would never want her. God, if she only knew. I crave her and everything she keeps trying to hand me. I crave her and everything she could give me. My very being calls out to her, and I work daily to refuse it.

So I pushed.

Until she ran.

But that ends right now.

Looking up at the gaudy neon lights thrown on the top of this hellhole, I know that was my first mistake.

*SYN.*

A motherfucking strip club.

This is not a place where my angel belongs. Just the thought of her inside this club makes my skin crawl. I can feel my anger becoming a force of its own as the blackness in my soul threatens to burst through. It's burning inside my veins and demanding blood. My nostrils flare, making my breaths come in loud pants. My fist clenches—demanding something to pound into, something to destroy. My skin feels tight. Every vein in my body is pulsing with each wild beat of my heart.

I'm going to explode.

The bouncer doesn't even give me a second thought. He gives me a brief glance as I pay the twenty bucks to gain my access into the hellish place. I immediately rip my sunglasses off, taking in every inch of the room. Black walls with dim lighting, stereotypical red carpeting and leather booths lining the room. They have the name right with the smell of this place—sex and sin with a mixture of smoke and sweat. There are three stages set up around the room, the center one being the largest and two smaller ones to the left and right, with a bar against the back wall and one on the top floor.

The whole top-floor bar area is set up on a glass floor, giving these douchebags around the room the perfect view between the barely dressed servers' legs. Taking my eyes off the top floor, where the bartenders are clearly working the glass floor to their advantage, I scan the room again, squinting my eyes to see through the dim lighting and heavy smoke.

That's when I spot her.

"What. The. Fuck," I snarl under my breath.

The anger I felt earlier burning through my body starts to boil. It's almost as if my body becomes a force of its own. The monsters inside me wanting free.

There she stands, not even five feet away, looking exhausted, wearing next to nothing. Her skirt—if that's what you want to call it—is more like a napkin someone cut in half. From the way she stands—slightly to the side—I can just make out the perfect roundness of her ass peeking out the bottom of the hem. Her pert tits are pushed together and held in a tight bikini top, the fabric so thin that I can see the outline of her nipples clear as day.

My eyes take in every inch of her exposed skin and I want to roar with rage.

No one should see her like this. No one but me. And even though I don't have the right to feel this way about her, there isn't a damn thing that can stop me now.

She hasn't seen me yet, so I stalk over to where she's standing.

She turns right when I'm about to reach out for her and her eyes go wide, shock and alarm clear in her beautiful, honey-brown eyes.

"Wha—"

"What the fuck are you doing, Em?" I bite out.

She shrinks back at my tone before she catches herself and goes stiff. I can tell instantly that I'm not going to like anything she has to say.

"Excuse me?"

"You heard me, Emmy. What in the hell are you doing in this place?"

She tilts her head slightly, taking me in. Her eyes leave mine and roam the room before she gives a stiff nod. When she turns her focus back to me, I go stock-still at her words.

"I'm exactly where I should be, Maddox. I'm home." Her tone is submissive, and that fury inside me goes from a boiling fire to ice cold.

With that, she turns and stalks off towards the bar. And I see that not only is her ass hanging out, but so are her hot-pink boy shorts.

"Dude. She's a fine piece of ass, right?" The man she was just talking to speaks in awe.

"Shut your fucking mouth," I growl, feeling that rage return like a switch has been flipped.

"Ah, you're new here. Just sit back, my friend, and get ready for the show." He laughs, takes a deep pull from his beer, and turns his attention back to the main stage, where the current entertainment is doing her best to swallow the fucking pole with her pussy. She's working so hard for it that she might as well be fucking the damn thing.

I'm no stranger to strip clubs. Back when the guys were all single, we would hit some local ones around California. No better way to let off some steam from the shit that is constantly swirling around in my head than to sit in a room full of naked woman. Where the music pounds into your body, the drinks are always flowing, and the pussy is in abundance.

One thing's for sure: This isn't a place for Emmy. Hell no.

Without taking my eyes from Emmy, I drop my body into the nearest booth. She's in a heated argument with the bartender and an older man who looks about as run-down as this fucking town. She throws her hands in the air, her head moving wildly, and if I had to guess, her stunning eyes are burning bright. She points over to me a few times, and all the older man does is shake his head, obviously not giving her what she wants. I just scowl at them from the booth, waiting for her to walk her ass back over here so I can explain to her that it's time to go.

"Hey there, handsome," a raspy voice says to my right. "Looking for some fun tonight? I bet a big man like you would be up for something wild."

"No." I don't even look at her. My eyes never leave Emmy—who is now looking at me. A mix of ire and hurt is written all over her face. Even with the shit lighting in this place, I can see it…and I hate it.

Fucking hurt? Is she serious right now? Pissed I can understand. She didn't want to be found and I found her.

"I won't bite, baby. That is unless you want me to." Her hands snake around my neck and down my chest.

Turning my attention away from Emmy, I look at the bleach-blonde hair, weathered skin, and fake tan of this bitch in front of me. I'll give her credit—she tries to hide it with more than enough makeup for about ten women, but this piece of work in front of me has to be pushing fifty.

"I said no, woman. What part of that didn't you understand? And for the last time, do not touch me." I reach up and pull her hand off my stomach before she can go any further.

Moving my eyes back to where I last saw Emmy has me coming up empty. What the hell? I scan the room but she is still nowhere to be found.

"Ah, sweet cheeks. I know what you want. Good luck with that one. Rose doesn't play around, and honey, why would you want her when you can have me? After all, I taught her everything she knows." She leans down and, before I can guess her intent, licks my neck, clearly taking my distraction at her words to her advantage.

I turn swiftly and move into her space, making sure she doesn't mix this shit up in her head to think that I would somehow ever want her ass.

"Do. Not. Touch. Me. You got that, *sweet cheeks*?"

She looks me in the eyes for a few beats before throwing her head back and laughing. The sound of it hits my ears like nails on a chalkboard.

"Your loss."

When she walks off, I start my scan of the room again. No Emmy in sight. I run my hand over my buzzed scalp before settling in for the wait.

Thirty minutes later and I still haven't found her. The crowd is getting restless. The chicks taking turns on the stage now haven't been impressive and they undoubtedly want more. The pole humper has moved on to one of the smaller stages. The last act on the main stage was slightly better, but all she did was basically finger-fuck herself on the stage before fumbling to get to her feet on her ridiculous heels.

Jesus Christ.

I wait, determined not to leave until I have her with me. Another thirty minutes and two more rotations on the stages have my frustration levels going up even higher. How the hell did she just disappear? I know she didn't leave. The tracking device on her car, which is sitting right next to my truck in the parking lot, hasn't alerted me of any movement. I'll be damned if she takes off on me again.

After signaling over another server, I order a beer and check my phone again to make sure the tracker isn't malfunctioning. I'm just putting my phone in my pocket when a deep voice cuts over the music.

"Gentleman of Syn. It's the moment you've been waiting for. The one your dicks have been begging for all fucking night. The Princess of Syn herself. The one and only, Rose!"

*The Princess of Syn? What an idiot.* I laugh to myself, placing my beer to my lips for a long pull. The music starts and the first few notes of Lollipop by Framing Hanley fill the air. Got to give this chick props—at least she picked a good song.

The house lights go down, plunging the room into darkness, before a spotlight hits the main stage. The smoke clinging to the air gives the stage an eerie glow. I take my eyes off the action and attempt scan the darkness of the room again for Emmy. Movement by the back corner catches my attention at the same time that the crowd goes electric. Idiots start throwing their money left and right, calling to this *Princess of Syn* to take them.

What morons.

I focus on the corner again and see the blonde from earlier smiling her wicked smile at me before pointing to the stage. Turning back to the stage, I watch as a woman, who I assume is this so-called princess, spins effortlessly on the pole, her movements all but blurring her body from the men wishing she were spinning on their dicks. It doesn't take me long to see why the bitch from earlier is telling me to look.

With one quick spin, her hands are placed at the center and her legs are spread wide and parallel to the pole, showing off her barely there G-sting, I see my Emmy. It takes a second for the shock to wear off, and in that second, she gracefully drops from her spin with a guarded smile to the men crowding the stage. Lifting her small hands from her side, she drags them up her flat stomach to take her tits in hand and jiggles them.

Fucking jiggles them.

I can't control my body at this point. I'm focused on one thing—the best way to get her off that stage and out of this place.

She reaches up and, in a move that is obviously practiced, removes her top, throwing it in to the crowd. There she dances with her body on display, caressing her naked tits until her nipples pebble. Turning her back to the room, she bends at the waist and starts to slowly pull her G-sting down her long, toned legs.

This is when the reality of this situation hits me. I'll fucking kill all of these motherfuckers in the room.

Then she drops to her knees before getting on all fours and crawling towards the end of the stage.

Hell. No.

I'm on my feet in seconds, stalking through the crowd, pushing any man who stands in the way of my woman and me. I don't even lift my arms from my side. I just barrel through the bodies with one goal in mind.

She doesn't see me coming since she's back on her feet and walking to the pole again. With a leap that would make my high school track coach proud, I'm on the stage, and a second later, I have a naked Emmy thrown over my shoulders before I jump off the stage. The sharp pain up my leg does nothing to extinguish my determination.

I can see the bouncers coming, and with one hand on her slick ass, I reach out and punch the first one in the face, taking great pleasure watching him instantly buckle to the floor. The other one comes at me from the side, but he doesn't get far before I pick up the chair to my left one-handed and crack it against his fucking head.

Emmy is struggling with such vigor that I'm forced to put her down. She looks up, ready to spit fire at me, before snapping her mouth shut when she sees the expression on my face. I have no doubt that I look just as feral as I feel.

"Don't you open that sweet fucking mouth, Emersyn. I swear to Christ, now is not the time to fucking piss me off any further."

I rip my shirt off and roughly pull it over her head. She struggles and puts up a fight, momentarily distracting me from the third bouncer coming at full throttle. His fist takes me by surprise, but not for long. Grabbing her wrist so she doesn't get away, I turn to the motherfucker stupid enough to get in my way.

"You shouldn't have done that," I seethe.

He goes to punch me again, but I duck and pop up before he

realizes he failed. Bringing my head forward, I head-butt him right between the eyes and almost smile when he falls instantly.

I'm stopped at the door by the last bartender she was speaking with earlier. He goes to make a move but pulls up when he sees the look in my eyes. I'll fucking kill and I'm sure it's written clear as day on my face.

"Do it. I dare you." My tone leaves no room for argument. I'm leaving with her and there isn't a person on this Earth who can stop me.

# CHAPTER 1
## *Emmy*

### PAST

"NO. NO, Emersyn. You can't spin like that. If you don't center your balance, the first thing that you'll end up doing is face-planting on the stage. You have to grip it like this," Ivy huffs with frustration.

We've been going over this damn trick for the last two hours. She's frustrated that I can't seem to pick it up. Oh, don't get me wrong. I can. I just don't want to. For some reason, I love annoying the hell out of her.

For as long as I can remember, I've been being 'groomed' to become the Princess of Syn, the strip club my parents own. Great parenting, right? Who has their kid doing pole tricks at ten? My parents do—that's who. They had me in just about every normal dance class I could take since I was old enough to move. Then it was time to learn the 'money makers,' as they call it. To them, this is completely normal. And this weekend, everything changes. I just turned twenty-one, and according to my mother, Ivy, it's time for me to stop serving the patrons and earn my keep.

"And remember, Emersyn, when you're on stage, you need to show them everything they're going to be begging for. No more of that shy shit. You already have The Ram pissed because you won't take the stage if he's in the room."

"Uh, seriously? Why would I take my clothes off if my father is in the room? You two are so jacked up."

Ivy squints her eyes at me. She hates it when I talk back. And she really hates that I refuse to do certain things when my own father is in the room. I'm sorry, but owner or not, there is no way I'm getting naked when The Ram—what Daddy dearest himself makes me call him—is in the room. That's just a whole level of icky that I don't want to deal with. It's bad enough that my mother has been teaching me how to take my clothes off and seduce men for years.

"Don't be an ungrateful brat, Emersyn. This whole place will be yours one day. These girls all see you and wish they could have parents that would hand them the world!" she screeches in my face. "Do the trick. And do it right this time or I'll have The Ram come in here and set you straight."

"Whatever," I mutter under my breath and roll my eyes.

Reaching up, I grasp the pole with both hands, careful to place them so that I have the most support for my small frame. Luckily, I was blessed with a body that makes this somewhat easier. I'm short, but what I lack in height I make up for in legs. My mother always said that I was lucky to have such great waist-huggers. Jesus, it's a miracle I'm not completely screwed up with the douche twins as my parents. After centering my body, I give a slight bounce, lifting my body horizontal to the stage, and use my momentum to spin. I hook one of my legs around the pole, using the heel of my five-inch stilettos to keep my balance.

"Come on, Emersyn. Use those abs and curl up. That's it. Now, grip it again with your hands before you spin out."

I can hear the pride in Ivy's voice from the fact that her daughter has mastered the trick she seems to think she's made famous. Really, I just climbed the damn pole with my legs and ground my vagina on the rod. It's gross. And I hate every second of it.

Right before I'm about to end the trick and land on my feet, I feel *his* eyes on me. Shawn. My father's head of security and, as I've been told by my mother and father…my future. The Ram's been grooming Shawn right alongside me so that he can marry his daughter off and sit back to enjoy his douchebaggery. Really, those two combined have a level of douchiness that could clean a vagina better than Summer's Eve.

I've hated Shawn since the first day his perverted eyes basically undressed my ten-year-old body. He is fifteen years older than I am, and there is nothing that makes him craving me as a young girl okay. It only continued to get worse the older I got. The Ram didn't even blink when I told him that Shawn had tried to force himself on me one day. He literally laughed in my face and told me, 'Well, Emersyn, do you blame him?'

Shawn would maybe be a somewhat attractive man if it weren't for the fact that he looks like a mob lord. He's a good foot taller than my five-foot-five frame. Solid muscles and so much chest hair that, when he wears his signature V-necks, it puffs through the opening like some disgusting fur rug. All he's missing is the thick, gold chains. He's attractive enough. I'll give him that much. Strong jaw, full head of black hair, shaped brows, perfectly doctored nose, and full lips. He's—minus the fur—the picture of male perfection. However, he repulses me.

I don't know what makes me do it. Maybe it's the fact that Ivy seems to think I have no idea what I'm doing. Maybe it's the fact that I hate what is going to become my life when I take the stage. Or maybe it's the fact that king douche himself, Shawn, is standing in the corner, rubbing his dick through his slacks. But I take over the stage in moves that I'm sure Ivy has never even dreamed of. I climb to the top of the ten-foot pole before doing the death drop to the bottom, ending in a split then using my hands only to climb back to the top. I use every ounce of my upper-body strength to work that pole. It becomes an extension to my body as I effortlessly dance. By the time I do my last spin, my body is pulsing with power.

I might hate my life and what I've been forced to live, but if this is all that's left for my future, then I'm going to own it the best I can. That is until the day I can find my out. Find a way to escape this madness before I lose hope that there is something better out there for me.

I won't let this break me. I'm stronger than that. I'm Emersyn Rose Keeze, the Princess of Syn, and one day, when I break free of this life, I'll be a better person because of what I have had to overcome. I won't let this define me.

"Well, well… Was that for me, Emersyn?" His voice makes me want to puke. Thick, deep, and full of sexual undertones. He makes no secret that he wants me with an unhealthy desire.

"No, Shawn. That was so that Ivy would shut up and let me get off that damn stage. Definitely not for you." I roll my eyes, feeling the power of his glare beating into my naked back. "Leave the dressing room. Now."

His hand reaches out and forcefully grips my forearms, pulling me back to crash against his chest.

"Let go of me, asshole. You know The Ram won't like it if you bruise up his fucking Princess of Syn. How will you explain that one?"

"You little brat. You think you have the control here? You think that little princess shit means anything to me? The Ram will pat me on the back for putting you in your place." His warm breath against my neck makes me want to vomit. God, he's disgusting.

"Fuck you," I spit.

"Gladly, Emersyn. Fucking gladly."

I'll give him credit. He proved me wrong that day. I put up a good fight, but anything that had been left of my innocence was stolen from me that day, and even though I knew I would eventually get out, something broke inside me. Whether it was the belief that I could overcome this life, the knowledge that I had in thinking I could escape unharmed, or the fact that every second I'd lived leading up to being roughly raped in the back dressing room of my family's strip club delivered home the fact that I'm nothing but trash.

Don't get me wrong. I know I'm worth more than this life I unfortunately was born into, but something about that day will forever taint a part of my soul. I've worked so hard to keep my mind closed off from the filth that surrounds me. The mother who thinks of me as some fucked-up version of herself to relive her life through. The father who looks at me, his own flesh and blood, as an object to make him money. And the man they've promised me to. This life that has been predetermined since they found out my dad's top dancer and piece of ass was having his daughter. The name I was born into, Emersyn, Locus City's Princess of Syn, the hottest and seediest strip club in south Florida. Since that fateful day The Ram forgot to pull out of Ivy, I've been destined to take the stage. And like it or not, it's all I have, and it's going to be my ticket out of this hell.

# CHAPTER 2
## *Maddox*
### PAST

"BABE," I whisper across her skin, pulling the sheet back as I kiss down her naked back. "Time to wake up."

I continue softly kissing down her spine, enjoying the fact that, even in her sleep, her body is responding to me. Goose bumps dance across her creamy skin, and when my breath dances across her body, she shudders slightly.

"Not yet. I'm too tired," she whines.

I let out a soft chuckle against the small of her back before nipping her ass with a soft bite. She moans but continues to doze.

"Mercy, baby, it's time to go or we're going to be late. It's my last weekend here before I ship out, and as much as I would love to spend that time deep within you, we have places to be." Even if those places aren't any I particularly want to be.

She starts to protest, but I dig my fingers into her ribs and laugh when she starts squealing like a pig and all but falls out of the bed to get away from me. God, she's beautiful in the morning. Her almost-white blond hair is a mess of soft curls, most likely from my grabbing handfuls of it all night. Her porcelain skin is glowing, my whisker burns showing up around her neck, tits, and thighs. Her sapphire eyes are bright with mirth. God, it feels good to see her like this. The last couple of weeks have left a sense of impending dread thick on my skin, but seeing her like this gives me hope. Hope that we aren't drifting apart. That, even though I'm leaving, we're going to be okay. Enough hope that I can ignore that dread that still won't vanish.

Mercedes Hutchens has been my girlfriend for the last four years. We were friends before that for a few years, and when I decided to take a chance, she became my girl. And now, my fiancée. Yeah, I'm a lucky son of a bitch.

It's been hard on us though. I'm deployed more than I'm home, and I'm about to leave again. I know it's even harder on her. Especially since I can't tell her where I go when I leave her sitting at home hoping and praying that I'll return to her. She knows as much as I can tell her. My team, which is made up of seven of the baddest motherfuckers from all over the United States, goes in hot to the deepest pits of hell. We have days to prepare, sometimes for months, but one thing is always clear. We don't fucking speak about shit.

I've been doing this shit since I turned eighteen and got the hell out of my house. And more specifically, got the hell away from Diana Locke. There isn't anything about my mother that isn't toxic. She's hated me since I was a snot-nosed brat. Not my brother, Mason The Perfect, but me—just for being alive. Forever reminding me that everything I touch is tainted with the blackness she sees in my eyes.

Mason and I, we are not close, and we probably never will be. She's made the perfect Stepford son out of him, teaching him everything she knows—including how to hate me. Being the heirs to our mother's family's oil business makes them just about the most powerful assholes in Texas.

My sperm donor of a father—Diana's words, not mine—ran out on her two months after I was born. Ever since, I've never understood the deep hate she has for me. Hell, I was a baby. There isn't really much I can do about her husband running out on her. Mason was five when I was born. The silver spoon was still attached to his mouth, and he's so far up my mother's ass that I'm convinced she never cut the umbilical cord.

So I got out and away from that life. With Mercedes's blessing, I joined the Marines, where I've been in control of my own life since the fateful day I left it all behind.

Sure, I can't give Mercy a life as glamorous as it would be if I would have stuck with Locke family tradition, gotten my Ivy League education, and started working for Locke Oil. We live in a small, one-bedroom apartment and drive used cars, and the rock sitting on her finger is about a tenth of the size she deserves. This might not be the life she envisioned, but I consider myself lucky to have her by my side and that she is willing to settle for less.

We're happy and that's all that matters. *Yeah, right,* that voice of dread reminds me. *You don't believe that—not with how she's been so closed off lately.*

"Why must we go over there, Maddox? You hate your mother." Her lip comes out in a pout that makes me want to nibble on its plumpness.

"Because, baby, she made it very clear that my presence is required for whatever reason, and with my trust shares in the company being turned over to me this month, I'm not crossing her in any way. Who knows what the troll has up her sleeve? But I'm not chancing that she takes our money."

Mercedes smiles at the mention of my trust. I've been waiting until the shares of the company, something my grandfather made ironclad, are unlocked so that I can have my mother or brother buy me out. I know she's been stressed about having to pick up a second job with me leaving. I hate that she has to work so fucking hard, but at this point, we don't have a choice. She doesn't have anyone other than me.

"All right. Will…will your brother and his horrible wife be there?" She avoids my eyes.

I hate that she has to fear my brother's wife. I've never understood her dislike for Mason's wife. From what I can tell, Josephine is the polar opposite of my mother and brother.

"I'm not sure, babe. Don't worry about them though, yeah?" I lift her chin and kiss her deeply before jumping off the bed, throwing her naked body over my shoulder, and taking her to the bathroom. If we're about to suffer through family time at the Locke mansion, then we might as well get satisfied first.

Yeah, life is pretty damn perfect.

My skin starts to crawl the second the gates open to my family estate. I can see Mason's shiny, black Aston Martin parked in front of the house. Every time I see his perfectly polished car, I have to fight the urge to run my keys along the frame. Luckily, that bastard is nowhere in sight. God, I hate being here.

I pull my fifteen-year-old truck to a clanking stop behind his car and I feel humiliated of what I can't give Mercedes. She should be in the best money can buy, but here she is, pulling up to another reminder of what I failed to give her.

"Let's get this over with, Mercy. I'm ready to get the hell out of here already."

She gives me a soft smile, but her eyes are telling me everything I need to know. There's a mixture of worry and fear dancing across the surface and something else I can't quite name. Shame washes over my body, but I choke it back and climb from the cab. Once I walk over to her, I help her down before we turn to face the Queen Bitch of Texas herself.

"Well, well…if it isn't my wayward son. Maddox," she bites out in way of greeting. Her eyes are already glossed over. I'm guessing she decided to hit the bottle early today.

"Mother." I have to stop myself from bowing at her feet.

"Mercedes. Pleasure, I'm sure." She gives her a calculated, wicked smile before turning her attention back to me. "Your brother is waiting for us in the study, and do hurry. We've been waiting."

"We wouldn't want to keep your precious Mason waiting now, would we?"

She snarls before slapping me across the face. I don't even feel it anymore. Years and years at the receiving end of her mental and physical abuse is enough that I can pretty much expect to be slapped a few times every time I'm in her presence. Mercedes's hand flinches in my hold, but I squeeze it to let her know that I'm okay.

"Don't you dare speak about your brother that way, Maddox. At least he is making something of himself. He isn't off playing G.I. Joe for some thrill. He isn't fucking trash." She gives me a few beats of her ice-cold glare, her eyes so dark brown they look black.

Just like mine. "Eyes of the fucking devil," she used to say to me.

"Forgive me. I wouldn't want to upset him, Diana."

"You bastard. Know your place when you're in MY house. I will be spoken to with respect, and so will your brother. And try not to ruin anything while you're here. In fact, you should just not touch anything. God forbid you taint our lives longer than necessary."

I give her a tight nod before following her through the white marble maze of her house. We reach the study and she takes a deep breath before opening the doors.

And there he is—the saint of our mother's world.

"Well, well, Maddox. You decided to come up from the slums to grace us today, I see." He laughs to himself before lifting his glass of amber-colored liquor to his lips.

His hazel eyes go to my left and I watch as he takes in all that is my Mercedes. I want nothing more than to bash his head in for looking at her that way, but I grind my teeth and steady my breathing. The quicker we get this over with, the better.

"Sit, Maddox," Diana says.

"I'm not a fucking dog," I growl.

"Yes, because you've proven otherwise with your deplorable behavior so far today."

"I'm here. I haven't done anything other than show up, and if that's *deplorable*, Mother, then I deeply apologize," I say. Mercy gives me a soft squeeze, reminding me to keep my cool. "Right. What was so important that I was required to stop by?"

She glares at me for a few moments before clearing her throat and looking over to Mason. I'm one hundred percent sure that Mason is the one running this farce now.

"Your brother and that terrible wife of his have decided to divorce. Unfortunately, this is going to put some strain on him for the foreseeable future. His money, the company money, is going to be frozen so that gold-digging little shit can't get her hands on it. That also means your shares in the company. Until we can get everything in order, that is."

"What the fuck!" I yell. "You can't do that. You don't have control over my trust."

Her eyes light and she laughs. "That's where you're wrong, dear boy. We had a clause put in that, if we feel like you're unstable or that your life and those you are surrounding yourself with are unstable, the shares in the company that would have become yours at twenty-five go into my control until I deem you stable enough to release them back to you. And honestly, Maddox, with you about to leave again—for god knows what and where—I don't feel like you have the best interest of the company. If you cared about the company and the trust you've been given of twenty-five percent of Locke Oil, then you would be doing the right thing and not playing little war games." She turns back to Mason, and not for the first time in my life, I want to grab her by the back of her hair and teach her a thing or two about who is in control of my life. "But that's neither here nor there now." Her smile is nothing short of pure evil.

"It really is a shame, brother, that you don't pay more attention to the paperwork that the family lawyers send over to you," he laughs, his eyes going back to Mercedes.

I try to remember what he's talking about but keep coming up blank. Shock and outrage that I'm once again being quite literally fucked by my own family is making it hard for me to concentrate.

"Think hard, little boy. Remember when Jefferson brought

you all those papers to sign? Prenuptial agreements for your precious Mercedes to sign in light of your *engagement.*"

I growl at Masons mention of Mercedes. They can treat me however they want, but I won't let them hurt her.

"Oh, did I make you mad?" He throws his head back and lets out a hardy laugh. "You really are a complete jarhead now."

My vision is starting to darken and I can feel the energy coming off me in waves. I want blood. I want to smash the smug-looking grins off their faces. The ones that tell me, once again, that they have won. I'm powerless when it comes to them and I fucking hate it. The last thing I need to be stressing about before I'm shipping out is this bullshit. I need my head clear. I need to be focused. And with just a five-minute conversation, they've blown that all to shit.

"I want to speak to Jefferson." My voice sounds foreign even to my own ears. The rage inside me is coming to a spilling point, and it's taking everything I have in my not to go apeshit.

"And what do you think Jefferson can do for *you*, Maddox? He's our lawyer, and unless you have some hidden money in your thrift-store furniture at home, I doubt you can even afford the cost to call him on the phone." My mother laughs at her dig.

She's right though. I have nothing to fight with. And since I'm leaving in less than a week, there isn't any time to fix this until I get home. I look over at Mercedes to find her staring at Mason with an expression that I can't understand. I clear my throat and she jumps at the sound. Looking over at me, she gives me a small smile and shrugs her shoulders. She's never been one to jump into confrontation, which is another reason I've worked so hard to keep her away from my mother and brother.

"This isn't over," I tell them.

“That’s where you’re wrong, brother,” he says with a hard tone to his usual indifference towards me.

He takes a few steps towards where I’m standing, coming toe to toe with me. I look into the face so different to my own. Where I’m tan skin, black hair, and even blacker eyes, he is the complete opposite. Light-brown hair, hazel eyes, and pale skin. How have I never noticed the menacing darkness that swirls around him?

“Check. Mate,” he snarls under his breath.

“You motherfucking bastard,” I yell, slamming my fist into his face.

He staggers back, wipes the blood from the corner of his mouth, and laughs. He laughs in my face.

“I might be a bastard, Maddox, but right now, I’m a bastard that has complete control over you, and you will do best to remember your place. Have fun on your little trip. I trust you two can see yourselves out?”

He turns his back and I watch as my mother rushes to his side and fusses over her baby. With nothing but rage coursing through my body, the monsters my family has planted into my very soul get a little larger.

Mercedes does her best to calm me down, but I know that they’ve won. There’s no way I’ll get my shares of the company. And all because I was stupid enough not to read the paperwork Jefferson sent over, assuming it was all the legal bullshit that came with protecting the company with my engagement and upcoming marriage to Mercedes. I should have known. I should have seen it coming. But I let the hopes that my darkness was finally getting a little brighter cloud my judgment.

“It’s going to be okay, Maddox. We can get past this,” she coos when we get back into my piece-of-shit truck.

"Yeah, Mercy? How exactly will we do that? We're barely staying afloat now. You're going to have to do better at the spending. We can't be wasting every check I get on more designer purses and shit."

"I…I can try, Maddox. But there are things we are going to have to buy now."

She smiles when I look at her, confused.

"I didn't want to tell you, but I think you need something to look forward to now that…well, now. I'm pregnant. We're going to have a baby." She smiles shyly and looks down at her hands.

A baby. Jesus. I can't even provide for both of us, and now, we have someone else to add to the mix. Every spare dollar we have she spends on more clothes and shit. I never minded—if she's happy, I'm happy. But now? A baby.

I sit there, running every possible scenario through my mind. I'll be gone for the next six months at best. She can't work two jobs that long. How the hell are we going to handle this?

"Aren't you happy?" she asks, looking at me, her face oddly void of emotion.

I clear my throat. "Yeah, babe. I'm happy," I lie. I love her, and somehow, I'll make this work—even if I have to sell my soul to the devil.

Four days later, I kiss my girl goodbye and never imagine that everything I've known for the last seven years was just a small piece in the giant game that's been playing against me. I leave distracted, worried, and—for the first time ever—afraid of what the future holds. I've worked so hard to give Mercedes a life she deserves. I should have known that the evil inside me would allow her to be tempted.

And unfortunately, when I need her the most, I'm denied even that.

Two months later, my war against my demons, the evil that I've always been told is deep within me, wins. And I'm left with even less than I came into this world with.

A broken man.

A broken man not worthy of anything pure in this world.

After all—everything I touch turns to shit anyway.

# CHAPTER 3
## Maddox

### PAST

"JOHNSON! GET fucking down! Morris, goddamn it, fall back!" I scream seconds before the earth shakes and a wave of fiery heat pulses through my body. Then I'm lifted off my feet and tossed like a rag doll.

When I'm able to clear my head a little, it sounds like I'm at the bottom of a tunnel and the air is whooshing around me. My eyes fight to open as I try to make sense of where I am. I can feel the sand blowing over my skin, prickling the exposed areas of my hands and face.

"John…" I struggle to get the word out, my lungs protesting and wetness bubbling up from my throat. I try to move my arm to wipe the annoying path it leaves when it rolls down my neck, but the second I do, it's like the trigger my mind needs to let me *feel* is pulled. The pain that shoots from my arm seems to ping-pong around my body until it shoots out my head.

I try to speak again, but more wetness drools out the side of my mouth. Fuck! I have to get the hell up! Mentally telling myself that I need to man the fuck up, I use every ounce of strength I have to pull my body together. Each movement I make causes my mind to scream, demanding that I just lie the fuck down and let go. But something in the back of my head tells me that, if I don't move now, it's going to be too late.

Focusing my eyes around the dust-filled fog swirling around me, I briefly make out Johnson's prone form just feet away. When I move to stand, I realize quickly why my body is telling me to just stop—my foot and a good part of my shin are all but hanging from my leg. I lie back and pull my belt from the loops, knowing that this is going to hurt more than I could ever imagine. Then I use what I can to secure my leg to minimize the damage. Inside my head, I'm screaming, but I know I need to do what's necessary. What I'm trained to do. I have to stop a few times just to keep myself from blacking out—the pain is that intense.

When I can finally see through the dust and pain enough to make out the best path to Johnson, my body is on the edge of losing consciousness. The pain is climbing higher and higher.

With my leg useless to handle my weight, I flip to my stomach and make the painful crawl forward. It takes way too long to get to Johnson, and I know that, if I don't hurry the fuck up, none of us will make it out of here. The car that exploded just seconds before could start a chain reaction with the two that are parked next to it. Not only that, but you can never assume that the area is free of more danger than just a car bomb.

The streets were empty when we made our way in earlier, but I saw the threat just seconds before the homemade bomb was triggered. Before I could scream out my warning—it was too late.

"Johnson, you hear me, brother?" I wheeze when I get to his side.

He doesn't respond, and after checking for a pulse, I know he needs a medic immediately. Before I assess the situation further, I look around for Morris. He was closest to the blast, but until I know for sure, I won't leave either of them behind.

I'm about to give up hope when I see him, and I know there is no way possible that he's alive. There is a large piece of metal impaling him directly through the chest.

Swallowing the lump in my throat, I crawl as quickly as my mangled body allows towards him and drag him back with me, moving away from the flames.

It takes me what feels like weeks in between bouts of vomiting my own blood, stopping numerous times during our evacuation to fire round after round at the camouflaged threat around us, and having to pause because my vision is starting to tunnel in and out, but I manage to pull my brothers for almost a mile before I hear the motor of an incoming truck. With no choice but to keep my path, I can only pray that it's one of our own. They know by now that help was needed. With signals down, I was unable to call it in, but there is no fucking way they missed that explosion.

I vaguely hear orders being called out and feet rushing around. The only thing I can think is, *Thank fuck they're American*, before I pass out.

# CHAPTER 4
## *Maddox*

### PAST

THE FIRST thing I feel when I start to wake up is pain. An unbearable pain I never thought possible is searing through my whole body. My eyes hurt, my arm is killing me, and my ribs and chest scream with every breath I attempt to take, but the worst pain is coming from my leg.

What the hell happened to me? I try to remember where I was last, but my head seems to be filled with nothing but dark holes. I attempt to open my eyes again, blinking fiercely at the pain from the bright lights.

I groan and try to move my arm to my eyes, coming up short when it smacks me in the head with a bone-crushing force. What the hell? Peeking through my eyelids, I see a bulky cast covering my arm from hand to shoulder.

Then it hits me. Johnson, Morris, and the bomb.

With a renewed rush of strength, I push my body to listen and open my eyes to look around the barren hospital room.

*Where the hell am I?*

I locate the call button and wait for someone to come and explain some things to me. Did Johnson make it? Did Morris's body make it home? Where am I? And why the hell am I in so much pain?

An hour later, I feel like my world is coming to an end. The only thing getting me through is the thought of Mercy and our child. The nurse just left with the promise to call my family—well, Mercy—and let her know that I'm awake. It's been almost a month since I got here.

As I fight the sleep that my body is demanding, I also battle with the fact that I've lost a chunk of my life. Numerous surgeries to mend my broken body have left me with a badly broken but healing arm, seven broken ribs, and one foot.

After the rest of our team found me dragging Johnson and Morris, we were taken the military outpost. I was airlifted to Landstuhl Regional Medical Center next to the US air base in Ramstein, Germany, as soon as I was stable enough to be moved.

Despite my best efforts, Johnson and Morris didn't make it. I can't even get past the part that I'm now going to have to learn how to walk again—not when my brothers didn't make it out alive. All because I was fucked up in the head from my problems at home. I missed the danger, and because of that, their families are husbandless and fatherless.

Hours later, I wake with a jolt. It takes me a second to realize that the screaming echoing throughout the room is coming from my own mouth. I'm soaked through with sweat from my nightmare of the bombing, but what has me screaming isn't reliving that hell. No, what woke me is the sensation that my foot is being sawed off. My whole leg feels like I've dipped it into a shredder.

"FUCK!" I scream, doing my best to get the covers off my feverish body. "Goddamn it!" I hear the heart monitor screaming as I force my body to move. To get to my leg before the pain becomes too much to bear.

After throwing back the covers, I reach down with the arm not in a cast and come up empty. The pain is getting worse with each second, but when I look down, there is nothing. Nothing but a covered stump halfway down from my knee. I scream from pain so uncontrollably violent that I start to vomit all over myself and frantically search for a way to turn off the feelings coming from a foot that is no longer part of my body.

A month later, marking seven months since I've been away from home, I've become used to the nightmares that wake me in pain to search for my missing foot. My wails have become a constant companion for the emptiness that's become my life. I fight with the depression that has settled over my body like a thick blanket.

The depression didn't sink in until I got a letter from Mary, Johnson's widow, telling me to stop trying to contact her family. The blame for her husband's death is all mine. By allowing myself close to him, her, and their kids, I have ruined their lives.

*"It should have been you, Maddox. I would have my husband and my children would have their father had you not failed them. I will never forgive you for ruining my life."*

Her words are a constant companion. I wake alone and I go to sleep alone.

The majority of my time is spent making sure the rest of my

body doesn't succumb to the darkness swirling around me. Doctors in and out, nurses, physical therapists—you name it. My room has become a revolving door of medical personnel. There's one thing that is painfully missing from this time.

Mercy.

She was notified. I know that much. But she hasn't come. Didn't even pick up when I called her over and over. My letters come back unopened. My own mother and brother didn't even care—not that I'm shocked there—but Mercy? My *Mercy* against the world I've been fighting since birth is gone, just gone. The hope is eclipsed more and more each day she isn't here.

"Well don't you look like shit," a deep voice jokes from the doorway.

I turn my head and lock eyes with Reid. He's part of my team, but he wasn't with me out on the field. He and the other men were clearing another part of the area when we took the other.

"Won't be winning any beauty contest. That's for fucking sure," Beck says, coming in behind him.

"Coop and Cage are on the way. We're getting the hell out of here and taking you with us. Time to go home and get the fuck out of this bed," Reid says. He gives me a lopsided smile, trying to ease some of the thickness in the air.

"Have you been able to get Mercy?" I ask. I don't give a damn about anything else right now. I need my girl. I need to know that she and our child are okay. Everything I've been pushing my body to do since the day I woke has been for her. I'll get stronger; I'll overcome—for them.

"Yeah, brother, we have," he says weakly.

Beck won't meet my eyes, and that damn sense of dread starts to fall over me.

"What the fuck does that mean?"

"Why don't we focus on getting you Stateside and walking again?" Reid tries to change the subject, his green eyes boring into mine.

"Tell me where the hell she is, Reid."

He flinches but doesn't say anything. Until I hear the voice I hoped I wouldn't have the displeasure of hearing again for a long time break through the silence.

"Oh you really are such stupid boy." She clicks her tongue. "They're not telling you because they seem to think you need to be eased into the news." She laughs. "I would ask how you are, but it looks like that demon seed that made you finally started to nip away at you. Quite literally."

"You fucking bitch," Cage sneers from the doorway behind my mother.

"No need for name-calling, dear. I'm just here to make sure there isn't anything tying me responsible for the invalid now that it's time for him to be discharged. Can't have that now. He's all yours, little boy." She pats Cage on the chest a few times before walking into the room. "It was such a long flight. Let me sit for a second before I tell you a little bedtime story." She walks over to where Beck's leaning back and gaping at her in the room's only chair. "Up now," she demands with a flick of her wrist.

Beck, being the lover and not fighter of the group, stands without argument and moves out of her way.

She sits, dusting off her black pants with her hands before folding them in her lap. I look up and meet her hard gaze, staring her straight on, refusing to let her see any weakness in me.

"Story time, bastard son of mine." She pauses—I'm sure for dramatic flare. "Once upon a time, there was a son born out of an accidental affair with the pool boy. Such a terrible decision on the mother's end, being that she was married with a perfect little angel already. Oh, and that her husband couldn't have more children. Imagine the scandal that rocked the house when she became pregnant. Of course, the husband was deeply confused, determined to stand by her side while the mother worked her magic and had her husband believing in miracles."

She laughs before her face falls and becomes serious again. "But that little bastard was nothing but trouble from day one. The mother was sick for the whole pregnancy, convinced that she was going to die from the demon inside her body. Her little prince suffered because she was feeling too unwell to care for him. Her husband—that miracle-believing fool—finally found out the truth when the baby was born. He looked nothing like his wife or other son, but instead favoring the dark complexion of a member of their staff. It was quite the time. Sure, that little bastard looked a little like his mother, but the differences were too vast for her lie to be believed. Like a thief in the night, her husband was gone."

She pauses while I struggle to keep up with what is obviously my life story. Sure, I've always been a little tanner than the rest of the family, but I share my mother's dark eyes and black hair. I always assumed that my brother just took after our father.

Holy shit.

"Ah, I see it's sinking in now. Yes, Maddox, you are that little bastard. The rotten little baby that was," she laughs. "Now here is where things get real fun. Your father, leaving when he did and proving that I had in fact been unfaithful, took oh so much from me. He took money that was rightfully mine. He didn't get my company, but even that was struggling. I've been fighting hard to build it back up for years. I knew that, one day, because of the way my foolish father had worded his last will and testaments, my sons would retain partial control of Locke Oil. I couldn't take the chance that your rotten hands would touch what is ours. You played right into my hands when you met little Mercedes. She's been of great importance the last few years." She pause, and I feel the urge to throw up.

Mercedes? What does she have to do with this fucked-up tale?

I look up and lock eyes with the four other men listening to this shit—each of them wearing the same expression of shock and outrage.

"I'm sure that, at some point in your ridiculously long relationship, she might have cared a little. It didn't take us much to persuade her to come work for our side of things. The money and power you can't provide her with can persuade even the strongest of souls. And of course it didn't hurt that your brother is quite fond of her. We offered her the world, something you would have never been able to give her. It was all planned out. All we had to do was wait for her to get that pathetic ring on her finger, have all those prenuptial papers drafted with the additional paperwork that relinquished your right to anything Locke Oil related, and wait for you to leave for another little game in the sandbox."

"The fuck you say!" Coop shouts, startling her enough to flinch.

"Hush, boy," she scolds.

"I got your fucking boy," he crudely yells back, grabbing his crotch.

"Let her finish," I interrupt before Coop can start bellowing again.

"Oh yes. We are getting to the best part. And the reason that I just sat on that dreadful plane. It really is a pity that you made it out alive. I'm not sure how you're going to be able to face the fact that, once again, your vile soul has tainted more lives. Those poor men…dying because of you."

Coop isn't the only one who lashes out at that. I hear them all start to yell over each other. I just sit there and stare her in the eyes, refusing to give her what she wants—my pain.

"As I was saying," she continues. "Since the day you were conceived, you have destroyed everything you touch. Every relationship in direct contact with you suffers. It wasn't enough that my husband left me, cleaning me out and making it so we couldn't have the best of the best. Mason had to suffer the disgusting public school system for years before I rebuilt our empire. You have been nothing but trouble from the beginning. Always doing something ridiculously careless in school. The early drinking and partying. And then disgracing the family by joining the military. Everything you have ever touched is shit, and Mercedes is lucky that she and my grandson got out when they did. Enjoy what's left of your life, Maddox." She goes to stand, and her words hit me like a Mack truck.

"Hey!" I scream when she is halfway through the room, walking fearlessly through the testosterone-driven minefield. "That's my son and I won't let her keep him from me!"

Judging by her smile, I would guess that my reaction is just what she was hoping for. After all, how would she dig the knife deeper if I hadn't spoken up?

"Oh, silly me. I forgot the best part of your bedtime story. He isn't yours. He's Mason's." She throws her head back and lets out an evil cackle. "That's right. Mason and Mercedes—they've been sleeping together for the last four years. They've been trying for a baby for the last two. Didn't you find it odd that the woman who made you wear a condom ended up pregnant? Took longer than they thought since she had to be careful not to show her hand to you and your brother had to finalize his divorce and all."

Before she leaves, she pushes her hand into her purse and throws something on my lap. Then she turns her back to my shocked face and clicks out the door on her heels.

She doesn't even spare her son a second thought as she takes off. How she can just so carelessly throw me away again and again will never make sense to me. Nevertheless, she's finally won. Taken everything I had left to live for and slapped me in the face with what she's been drilling into my head my whole life.

Everything and everyone I've ever touched has been ruined. The evilness she embodies and the demons that have been nipping at my heels since I started walking have won.

With nothing left to give, I pick up the item on my lap and feel that hope inside me die a painful death.

Mason, with his arms around Mercedes, is the first thing I see in the close-up shot. The second is the little baby in her arms. The little baby that looks nothing like me. Mason's son. I close my eyes and allow the only tear I'll ever shed over my life to roll down my cheek.

Never again. I will never allow myself to harm someone else.

I'm a broken man.

A broken man with black hole left where his heart used to be.

I'll get past this, but I will never open myself up to this kind of pain again.

A blessed life is something I have never known, so I'm not sure why I ever hoped to feel its glory.

# CHAPTER 5
## Emmy

### PAST

NIGHT AFTER night, all I have is the stage, my spotlight, and Shawn. Since the night he raped me in the back dressing room six months ago, things have gotten out of hand. The Ram just looks past his rough hands, and Ivy thinks it's just wonderful that I have such a strong and handsome man. When I tried to tell her that that 'strong and handsome man' was raping her daughter daily, she laughed. Told me that I needed to grow up and start learning how to please my man.

What the hell is wrong with these people?!

*It will be over soon,* I remind myself. That's the only thing that pushes me to keep going, to not give up. I've saved every single dollar I've made at Syn. Being the 'Princess of Syn' and knowing what the hell I'm doing when I take the stage have their benefits. They toss money to me left and right. I could leave tonight, but I want to get past this last weekend and get the high rollers who always hit Syn when it's the end of the month. Payday for most, and that's when the biggest money gets tossed onto my stage.

"You're up in ten, Rose!" Diamond yells as she rushes past me to go change, her huge, fake tits bouncing up and down.

The smell of her…arousal makes me gag. I'll never understand how she gets off stripping. I guess, for her, it's an exhibition type thing. She loves being watched. Not for me though. I hate showing all these men my body. That's why I demand that the house lights get turned down and only a spotlight. It shields them from me in a way. I get up there and try to forget that I'm dancing naked for them. I let the music take over my body. At this point, it moves as if on autopilot. I go out there, do what is expected of me, and then take my money and run. Usually, I just run right into another piece of my hell.

Shawn.

Over the last month, he has become more and more violent, his hands leaving bruises against my arms and hips. Recently, he's left them around my neck, causing me to get creative with my makeup. I stopped fighting him a while back—when it became clear that he got off on my struggles. I have a feeling that his escalated roughness is because he *wants* me to fight. I just don't care anymore. I'm so close to leaving that there isn't much more he can do to damage me.

He's already taken so much, and I refuse to give him my pride. I'll hold on to that until my dying breath.

It's almost time. I'll escape this hell, and when I do, I'm never going to look back.

MY MUSIC is just coming to the end. I do my last rotation of the stage, making sure that my naked body is on display to every one of the men pulled up to the stage. Their shouts are almost loud enough to drown out the beat of my music.

I let my legs go and drop to a split, my pussy hitting the stage, and then I silently say my nightly prayer that I don't catch anything from the exposure. Dropping onto my back, my legs spread, I throw my head back in a mock pose of ecstasy before dragging my hands from my ankles to rest at the apex of my legs. Making sure all these idiots can see every bare inch of my sex.

The crowd goes electric. Crossing my legs, I roll and get to my knees, where I continue to play with my body. Seducing the crowd to give me every last dollar.

By the time the last note of my music hits my ears, the stage is so full of money that I can't even see the black flooring through the cash.

My escape.

It is worth every second of the humility I just endured.

I collect the money and stuff it into the bucket that Pearl tosses my way. Then she cleans off the pole as I finish cleaning my earnings off the stage.

"Thanks," I pant as I rush past her.

I have about two minutes to dump this money into the safe I keep in my locker before Shawn finds me. Not even giving a care to my nudity, especially since he will just pull anything I put on it my body off, I dump the bucket's contents into my safe and slam it shut.

I just know that tonight is the night I get the hell out of here.

"Emersyn, Emersyn, Emersyn. That was quite the show you put on tonight. If I didn't know better, I would think you actually enjoyed yourself out there." He comes up against my back. The cheap fabric of his suit roughly rubs against my oiled skin. "You going to fight me tonight, little Syn?" he rasps against my ear, biting my lobe. He's started asking this question each night he takes me.

And every night since, I've answered him the same way.

"In your dreams."

"One day, Emersyn. One day, when I have my ring on your finger and your dear old daddy gives me this club, you're going to learn where your fucking place is. Your fucking lippy mouth will only get you so far. The Ram might put up with it, but I sure as hell won't."

He grips my arms and spins me before pushing me against the lockers. The metal scrapes against my back, cutting it open in some spots, but I don't make a sound.

"Get on your knees and suck my dick, bitch," he demands.

I drop instantly, wondering in the back of my head if it's still rape now that I've stopped fighting him.

It doesn't take him long before he grabs both sides of my head and starts thrusting into my mouth with a bruising force.

"That's right. Take it all. Take all of Daddy's dick."

God, how repulsive can he get?

I attempt to keep my mind from engaging. I let my body take over and try to go to my happy place. When his hand curls around my neck, it becomes obvious why he started this new game. He wants my attention, and what a better way to get it than taking my air?

When he lifts me to my feet, his needle dick falls from my mouth and I struggle to control the fear at my lack of oxygen.

Roughly, he pushes me forward, causing me to crash into the table in the middle of the room. Makeup and clothing scatter around us as he lifts me, flips me, and then slams me onto my back. His hand goes back to my neck before he forcefully pushes into my body.

I'm on the verge of blacking out, his thrusts picking up speed, but then I finally come out of my head and grab ahold of his wrist with my hands. Trying desperately to get some much-needed air, I claw at his skin, begging with my eyes for him to let up.

"That's right, Emersyn. Fucking fight me," he pants, sweat beading around his forehead and rolling down his neck. "Fucking fight, bitch!" he screams into my face.

I'm seconds from passing out when I feel his body disappearing. I sit up, struggling to let the air in, and meet the crystal-blue eyes of my savior.

"You okay?" he asks.

I nod mutely. A million questions rush through my head, but not a single word escapes before he nods and slams his fist into Shawn's face. I want to weep when I watch him crumple to the floor, passed out cold.

"I'm Zeke, but my friends call me Coop. I know you don't know me, but I promise you can trust me. I was walking to the bathroom and I heard him…and, shit…" he trails off, running his hands through his thick, blond hair. "I'm not going to hurt you, but I would like to help if you'll let me."

I can't stop the tears if I wanted to. Silently, I nod, still not trusting myself to speak. Then I hastily throw my clothes on, open the safe, and shovel all the cash I have into my duffel bag. There's nothing else here I need.

"Come on. Let's get you out of here." He reaches out, my savior, and takes me out of my hell.

I don't look back once.

COOP TAKES me back to his hotel, helps me get cleaned up, and offers me some clean clothes that don't smell like an ashtray. He only leaves me long enough to get some bandages to clean up the cuts on my back. I'm not sure what it is about him that has me trusting him instantly. Maybe it's because, as far as options go, he's my best one. For all I know, he's some crazy serial killer and I'm playing right into his hands.

The whole time he dabs alcohol on my back, I don't utter a word. Not until he tells me that I won't ever have to go back there. I sharply turn my head and look right into his eyes before laughing.

"I have no where else to go. I have to go back."

He shakes his head and smiles. "Nah. I've got your back now. Chin up, buttercup. We're a team now."

TRUE TO his word, Coop became almost like a brother to me. He took me in and helped me get stronger. He had to go out to California, where he worked for a security company, but he made sure I was taken care of. They stayed busy and he hated leaving me alone, always worried that something would happen.

Six months after the momentous day he saved me from Shawn, he finally introduced me to Axel Reid, the owner of Corps Security, where Coop worked. Axel was apprehensive about hiring me since I was so young, but their company was growing so quickly, and college education or not, I'm now gratefully employed as a secretary for Corps Security.

For once, things are starting to look up. I have a great friend and a caring boss, and I wasn't scared. I've mapped out my five-year plan, and I'm finally allowing myself to dream. All of those dreams explode in my face when I finally come face to face with *him.*

"Uh…can I help you?" I ask the man standing in front of my desk.

"Name."

"Excuse me?"

His face remains expressionless. His dark eyes don't travel down to my chest like I've been used to over the years, but he keeps me tapped in his gaze. My body becomes more and more paralyzed with each passing second that I look at this man.

"Your name," he repeats.

"You want my name?" I stupidly reply.

One dark brow cocks without losing his stoic mask and he just waits. My cheeks heat and I have to fight my body's reaction to this man in front of me.

"Em…Emersyn. Emmy. I mean, I'm Emmy," I whisper.

He nods and then walks past my desk and down the hall.

It takes me a second to clear the unexpected fog of lust that is taking over my body. I jump up from my seat so quickly that it rolls into the wall behind me before I run after the tall, dark, stranger.

"Wait!" I yell.

He stops but doesn't turn.

"You can't just walk in here," I gasp at his back.

"It's fine, Emmy. That's Locke. He's our technical specialist. He's just been out of town." Beck says softly behind me.

I turn to gape at Beck, my mouth opening and closing like a guppy.

He just shakes his head and looks to where Locke is still standing with his back to us. "It's cool, Em. Just go on back to the front, okay?" He offers me a sad smile and turns to walk over to Locke.

I give him another glance, noticing how tense his body is strung. His hands are clenched in a firm fist and his shoulders are pulled tight.

I head back to the front, thinking about Locke. He's so intense. My body was on fire just from his eyes. He spoke three words to me and I'm already hooked.

It wasn't love at first sight, but I'm drawn to him. Even now, with him down the hall from me, I can feel my skin tingle with the memory of his black eyes holding my own.

With a smile, I return to my work and think to myself that my five-year plan just got a lot more interesting.

# CHAPTER 6
## Emmy

### PRESENT TIME

THAT SON of a bitch!

Who the hell does he think he is? For years, he's treated me with indifference. The only time I got past his thick shield was at Axel and Izzy's wedding. He had so much to drink that he doesn't even remember that he almost took me against the wall at the reception. Not one of my finest moments, but I savored those precious memories of his mouth and hands on my body. I'm not proud of it or what it makes me, but that small memory has carried me through some tough times lately.

Like a naïve little girl, I've harbored my crush on Maddox Locke since the first time I met him back in California. It took losing the one person I considered family to wake me the hell up. I've been panting after the one man who couldn't care less about me, giving him every second of my dreams, only to get pushed down each and every time. Sure, I've dated here and there, but no one has ever made me feel the way he did. It was hopeless.

Every since the day that Coop died, I feel like I've been struggling to find my place. Find where I belong. His death kills me daily. We weren't as close as we had been four years ago. Between things picking up at CS and our moving from California to Georgia, we were just too busy. I regret that daily. I know I looked stupid for running, but I couldn't stay. Not when I'd lost the one person who'd had my back like no one else. Sure, I was close with the girls—especially Melissa—but something held me back from giving them one hundred percent of Emersyn. To this day, the only ones who know my whole story are Axel and…well, Coop.

I'm sure the other guys know bits and pieces, but they don't know everything. Axel made me a promise the day I met him that he would do his best to never let my past come up again. I'll never forget his words.

"We all have our battles. We get past them the best we can by putting one foot in front of the other. Looking back doesn't do anything but make it hurt a little more."

So that's what I did. I did it for four years as I worked for the boys and then I did it again when Coop gave his life and saved me again.

One foot in front of the other.

"You have a lot of nerve, Maddox Locke," I deadpan.

He takes his eyes off the road and levels me with what I'm sure is meant to be one of his signature shut-the-hell-up glares. They don't work on me anymore. I don't care. He's kept me dangling by a string of desire for years now. I prayed that he would just look at me. And now, now that I'm working on fixing myself, he thinks he can just storm right in and save the day.

"What do you want from me? Huh? Is this some sick game with you?!"

He ignores me. Not that I expected anything less. But it does nothing but fuel my fire. How dare he!

"Four years, you idiot! I all but handed myself over to you. The only thing that was missing was a freaking bow and a cherry on the top! Four stupid years I wanted you. And now… What is this now? I'm not good enough for you, but you still want me to die a little inside by forcing me to be around you?"

His jaw ticks, but that's all I get.

"Answer me! Why! Why now?"

Nothing.

"I hate you!" I exclaim, hating the taste of those words from my mouth when directed him. I don't hate him and I probably never could. I'm not really sure what that says about me at this point.

I have to hold on to the dash when his car suddenly swerves to the shoulder and comes to a jarring halt. He doesn't move to face me. Hell, he doesn't move at all. He just faces forward with his white-knuckle grip on the wheel and his chest moving rapidly with each breath he forces through his nose.

But he still refuses to speak.

"I loved you once, you know," I whisper more to myself than to him, but he hears me because I watch his eyes close. "I loved you unconditionally even though I was—no, even though I *am*—nothing to you. I left because being around you and trying to get over the fact that I'm the reason why Coop is dead was just too much. I was dying, daily, every time you would look at me but look right through me. I'm not sure why I thought that you would somehow be there for me when you never had been before."

He doesn't say anything, instead choosing to remain silent and let my confession linger in the air. His eyes are still closed, his body pulled tight, reminding me of the first time I met him. Even all these years later, we're still no further than we were the first time we met when it just took three words for me to be hooked.

I let out a choppy breath and fist my hands tight, letting the pain of my nails take away the urge to cry. Gazing out the window, I beg myself to get it together.

I'm done crying over Maddox Locke.

*"Chin up, buttercup."* My chest hurts when I remember Coop's thing for me. He was constantly saying that to me when I was having a hard time.

I hear Maddox mumble under his breath and I turn my attention back to the driver's seat. He's looking at me with an expression I've never seen on his face before. I frown and let my eyes take in every inch of his face, attempting to place whatever he's trying to tell me with his eyes. I come up empty and sigh. Why did I think I would get anywhere with this man? I look away when he doesn't speak.

"You were never nothing, Emmy. Never nothing. Not to me. You've been *everything* for longer than I care to admit, but you deserved more than a poor bastard like me."

I almost miss his words, but my eyes snap back to his and my jaw drops.

"For such a smart man, you really are clueless. I never wanted anything *but* you. What I deserved was you not pushing me away like yesterday's trash. What I deserved was you treating me like a human being with feelings and not to play games with my heart."

"I never played games with you, Emmy. I just tried to get you to recognize a lost cause. I wouldn't be able to live with hurting you."

"Are you blind?! Jesus, Maddox! That's all you ever did was hurt me." I laugh without humor. Then I angrily swipe at the tear that sneaks past my demand to stay locked inside. "I don't want to talk about it right now. Just drive to wherever the hell you're determined to take me so I can get some sleep. We can talk about it later before you take me back to Syn and head home."

"I am home, Em," he says under his breath.

I have no desire to argue with him, so I just lean my head against the glass and work on my strength to get past the next stage in his game.

# CHAPTER 7
## Maddox

I PULL INTO the hotel, shut off the engine, and try to calm myself down. I've worked for over a decade to keep my emotions sealed away, determined not to let anyone in while I deal with the stone-cold truth that I ruin everything and everyone. I did exactly what she accused me of. I pushed her away. I was intentionally cruel to her by throwing other women in her face. Women I had no real taste for at all. Fillers, they were a means to a distraction. Let's face it—eleven years is a long fucking time to go without sex.

So I used them. Paraded them in front of Emmy when the few social settings we were in deemed it worthy. I'll never forget the look of pure agony the first time I brought one of them around. Daisy, a chick who knew that, when I called, all I needed was her to meet me at the local hotel and check in. She did me a favor and played the part, but all I got out of it was the feeling of sinking in the middle of the ocean with no boat in sight.

She's right; I played games to keep her from getting too close.

By trying to protect her, all I did was screw with her mind and hurt her anyway.

I look over at her sleeping form, and for the first time since we lost Coop and she ran, I allow myself to breathe without the fear holding me hostage. I let go of the bone-crushing thought that she's going to disappear and allow myself to *feel*. It would be easy to take what she was so willing to give me. To feel the blessing of her love shining on me.

With the floodgates open wide, I let the love I feel for this woman out. It will bring me to my knees if I let it. I don't *want* to keep pushing her away, but how do you take something that has been integrated into your mind for so long go and move on? How do you change your whole outlook on life with just a hope that everything you've ever experienced from those who should love you was wrong?

"Em?"

She doesn't even flinch. I remember that, when I saw her earlier, she looked exhausted. I know she's been dealing with a lot from losing Coop. Hell, we all have, but the Emmy I know is always so full of life.

After twisting from my seat and climbing from the car, I make my way over to her door. My leg has been driving me crazy this week, my stump getting sore from overuse, and I know I did too much with my stunt back at the club. I'm usually good about not overdoing it. I can go about my life almost the same as before, but sometimes, I have down moments. This is quickly becoming one of those times. All I want to do is get this thing off me.

She all but falls into my arms when I swing her door open. I adjust her and take the brunt of her weight, as slight as it may be, on my good side before making my way into the hotel. It's the nicest place I could find within a thirty-minute drive of Syn, and it's only five minutes away from the place she's been staying. I would have gotten something nicer, but I didn't want to be too far from her. It was bad enough that I hadn't physically seen her to make sure she was okay in weeks, so this was the best-case scenario for me.

I make the long walk to my room, struggle for a second to get the door open and not drop Em, and then settle her down on the bed. Not one second does she stir, showing me just how exhausted she really is.

Reaching out, I brush one of her honey-blond strands behind her ear. Her lips twitch and she sighs in her sleep. My heart picks up speed when she murmurs my name. Even in her sleep, she's completely devoted to me.

Why can't I let go of every fear I've ever known and trust that this might be the one person I don't completely screw up?

I make quick work of stripping off my clothes and removing my prosthetic. My leg is already feeling slightly better now that I know I'll be able to get off my feet for the night. I carefully move my body towards where she is curled into herself in the middle of the king-sized bed. She continues to sleep contentedly as I pull her into my body and yank the covers over our bodies. With as tired as she is, I just hope that I can catch a few hours of sleep before I need to put my leg back on. I don't want her to know before I have a chance to ease her into it. It's been my experience that, when they aren't prepared for it, the shock is greater, and as much as it hurts to think that she could have this reaction, they're sometimes disgusted by it. But, like it or not, it's part of who I am now, and if I'm going to let her in, then she needs to see me for me—flaws and all.

In all the years I've known her and dreamt about having her in my arms, there is nothing that could ever have prepared me for the sense of peace that settles my soul by having her here.

I SHOULD have known better than to let my guard down. I wake up screaming, the events that have haunted me nightly since I lost my leg playing out in an endless loop. Only this time, it isn't Morris's lifeless body I pull away—it's Emmy's. I never thought that nightmare would get worse until I envisioned her lying there, dead.

Gasping for air, I try to bring myself back from the tangled web of pain that always follows my nightmares. I try to remember that I'm not back *there*, I've overcome the aftermath of that dark day, and I'm in control now. I'm alive. Emmy is alive.

*FUCK! Emmy...*

As trepidation fills my veins with ice-cold fear, I look over to her and prepare myself for her revolution. I try to close off myself to what it will do if she hates me now—or worse, if she fears me. My world is rocked to its very core when I take in her pale, tear-streaked face. Her sobs are so violent that they're shaking the bed, and for the first time since she walked into my life, I have no idea what she's thinking.

We stare at each other for the longest time. She seems unsure of what to do and say. I'm terrified that, if I move, she's going to crack. Seeing the pain I've caused yet another person because of my demons is slowly killing me. I knew this would happen. I feared this. But despite my best efforts, here we are and she's seen me at my worst.

I surrender to the pain and drop my head, running my hand over my scalp and wishing that I hadn't shaved it off so that I would at least have something to pull. To make my body feel pain over my fucking heart.

When I feel her cold hand against my back, I jump, causing her to pull her arm back and cry harder.

"Please…please don't push me away, Maddox," she begs between her tears. "I can't help you if you don't let me in."

After whipping my head around, I hold her eyes and try to make sense of her words. Push her away? Jesus… I've never wanted more than to pull her into my arms and forget everything that weighs me down.

"Let. Me. In," she pleads. "Please let me in."

"God, Em. You've always been in."

She lets out a shuddered breath and takes a hesitant inch towards me. Her kneeling body moves slowly with the fear I've helped plant in her mind that I'll reject her. I've done this to her and I vow to do my best to never make her doubt my need for her.

Her hand comes up from the bed and extends out for me again, her palm caressing my cheek as she takes the last few scoots on her knees to reach me. My eyes never leave hers as I reach out and finally meet her in the middle. I can see the relief in her eyes when, for the first time in years, I take what she's been offering me. My arm goes behind her back, my hand lightly digging in when I curl it around her ribs and pull her into my chest.

She cries softly, and at this point, I'm not sure if it's because I've given her this moment or because she's still scared from my nightmare. Her small hands dig into the skin on my chest and it feels like she is trying to fuse our bodies together. I lean back against the pillows and let her have this time to calm down. After a few minutes of silence, she lifts up, her hands still firmly pressed against my chest, her eyes imploring.

"Em," I whisper, not sure where to even begin.

She doesn't even hesitate before reaching up and framing my head between her hands. Her thumbs take a sweep against my cheek before her lips press against mine. Hesitantly at first, unsure if I'm going to push her away, before allowing herself to take what she wants.

I reach out and pull her by her slim hips to straddle my waist, not even caring that there is nothing but my thin boxer briefs separating us. She moans when my erection presses against her core. The heat of her pussy settled against my lap is almost enough for me to come on the spot.

With a growl, I deepen the kiss, taking it to a level of predatory ownership. Our tongues swirl together, her breath mixing with my own and our mouths doing all the talking for us.

In this moment, she owns me. Everything I've been denying us both comes to a screeching halt.

I allow myself this moment. I allow her this moment and pray that, when the sun comes up in the morning, she doesn't hate me for pushing her away again.

# CHAPTER 8
## Emmy

WHEN I wake up to Maddox's screaming and shaking in the bed, my first thought is that I have to be dreaming. Then the events that led up to us being in the same bed come rushing back. It's been weeks since I've allowed myself just a second of rest, so it's not a shock that, the second I got around the one person who I know deep down would never let harm come to me, I crashed.

The noises that are coming from his throat are tearing me to pieces. I forget the hell that will be waiting for me when I return to Syn and focus on the broken man who needs me now. I just pray that he will let himself take what I so desperately offer him.

The second he lets his walls down and our lips meet, I know that every feeling I thought I would feel when he finally let me in isn't even a fraction of the reality. I feel alive for the first time in months. Hell, maybe for the first time in my life. When I decided to let him go, I never thought that this moment would come to fruition. I never let myself believe that it would happen.

His fingers curl into my hips, and I jump when he hits my sore spots—crying out when the pain rips through my middle.

And just like that, the moment is gone.

He pulls his mouth from mine and searches my eyes for the cause of my whimper. One clearly pain-derived and not because I can feel him hot against my core.

"Did I hurt you?"

I should lie. I know even before the words leave my lips that the moment is gone.

"It's nothing," I say in the hopes that he will drop it.

"You don't have a reaction like that over nothing, Emmy."

He snaps the light beside the bed on and gently pushes me back some from his chest. He lifts my shirt up at the hem, and I close my eyes when I feel his fingers trace the bruising around my sides. He is silent for the longest time, but I don't open my eyes.

"Who fucking did this to you?" His voice breaks through the silence, and just the sound of his rage makes me flinch.

"Maddox, please… It's nothing."

He leans in, his nose just inches from mine, and looks me in the eyes. "It isn't *nothing*, Emmy. There are goddamn handprints all over your hips. This is as far from nothing as it gets. I won't ask you again, Emmy. Who did this to you?"

I squirm in his lap, trying to get some distance from him, but his arms wrap around my middle and hold me hostage.

"It was an accident?"

His nostrils flare, and I watch as his eyes darken even more.

"I fell?"

His jaw ticks.

"I—"

"Swear to Christ, if you feed me another line of bullshit, I'll put you over my knee and spank your ass, Emersyn."

Holy shit.

"It was...Shawn." I sigh and cringe when I remember the night I came back to the club and the welcome home from him I got. I don't know why I thought that he would have left me alone. I might be older now, but with The Ram ready to retire, Shawn is even more powerful at the club. Ivy is still strutting her old ass around the floor like she's twenty. The Ram sticks to the bar or his office, not giving a damn about what goes on around him. Now that his Princess of Syn has come home licking her wounds, he could care less what happens as long as the money is flowing.

But Shawn. He is like a piece of gum you can't get off your shoe. The evil that was only simmering in him years before has now grown to insurmountable levels. He no longer cares who catches him fucking unwilling dancers in the back. Clearly, since he raped me the first night I had come back and didn't even stop when Ivy walked into the room. She looked right at my tear-streaked face and cocked her head like she couldn't understand what she was seeing. Shawn just laughed and took me harder.

"Who the fuck is Shawn?" he snarls.

How do I explain Shawn? "He-he's... I'm not sure how to answer that, Maddox," I tell him honestly.

"Explain," he demands.

I hold his eyes for a few beats before scooting off his lap and folding my legs next to where he is lying. "Shawn is the manager of Syn. The Ram—my father's right hand...and my worst nightmare."

The veins along his neck pulse with his anger as I wait him out, praying that he doesn't ask the questions I know will follow. I have wanted nothing more than him to open up to me, so it's only fair that I play by the same rules. Even if the truth is as ugly as it gets.

"You know my parents own Syn, right?" At his nod, I continue. "I was put into dance when I turned two. The cute little beginner classes every little girl dreams of taking," I laugh without mirth. "Those turned into advanced classes as the years went on. I've been trained in just about every form of dance there is. And all of that was for one thing—so that I would take over the club as headline dancer and my parents could sit back and keep making money. But according the The Ram, no princess can rule without her *prince*, and to him, my prince is Shawn."

"That doesn't explain how that motherfucker's handprints ended up all over your body."

I don't argue with him; it doesn't explain that. But I also don't know what he's going to do when I tell him the rest.

"Keep going," he stresses.

"I managed to put them off until I turned twenty-one. Don't ask me how because I'm still not sure, but the first night I took the stage seemed to be the green light for him to claim his princess. And every night until I was saved from there, until the night I came back. He continues to claim his princess."

"The hell you say?"

I just nod my head and move to leave the bed. Distance seems like a good idea right now.

"Don't you dare leave this bed."

I turn and almost fall to my ass when he pulls me back to him.

"He put his hands on you. That bastard hurt you. I'll fucking kill him," he vows, and I don't doubt that he means it.

"No, you won't."

"The hell you say!"

I roll my eyes at him, causing his to narrow. "I'm where I deserve to be, Maddox. We can chalk this night up to a lapse in judgment on your end, and come morning, you can drop me back off and go home."

"Are you serious? You think for one second that I'm willingly going to hand-deliver you to your piece-of-shit parents and a fucking rapist!" he bellows.

"That's exactly what you're going to do." I wiggle out of his hold and walk to the bathroom. I need to get my shit together and I can't do it when he's near me.

I stand under the scalding-hot water that's raining over my body and let my mind wander back to when I believed my love for Maddox could overcome everything. That seems like a lifetime ago when it was really just months earlier. He's pushed me away for so long that it almost feels like some twisted kind of normal for us, but it isn't fair to either of us to continue this tug-of-war.

I can't keep wishing for the impossible and he needs me to leave so he doesn't have some pathetic hanger-on. Coop would be pissed if he knew that I went back to Syn. I can't help but feel like I've, in a sense, let him down. He saved me from this life, took me in, and made sure I was safe. He gave his life for me. And I repaid him by jumping right back into the fire.

The grief I've felt over his death and my role in it comes crashing back over me and I drop to my knees. The water continues to beat over my skin as I let out the emotions I've been struggling with for weeks.

I owe him for so much and I never would have been able to pay him back, but I can't even remember the last time I hugged him and reminded him how thankful I was to have him in my life. I remember being frustrated with him because he had been acting like a jerk the day before. Not many people saw his serious side, but I did. He was yelling at me to get my thumb out of my ass and move on. He was always my biggest cheerleader, and it kills me to know that I'll never see his smile again. I'll never feel his strong arms comforting me after a hard day and the shadows of my past creep up on me.

"Em? Come on. Turn off the water and let's go."

I ignore him and sit back on my ass, tilting my head up and letting the water wash my sorrow away.

"Now."

"I'm not a dog, Maddox Locke! I don't come on command!" I shout over the water.

"Want to put money on that?"

That jerk!

I stand too quickly, and before I can catch myself, I'm tumbling through the curtain and onto the floor. Maddox, clearly not having anticipated my literally falling at his feet, moves back. The stoic mask I've grown so used to slips for a second and I see the shock followed quickly by lust before he hides again.

He comes out of his shock and helps me to my feet. Then he reaches over the counter and pulls a towel off before thrusting it into my arms and leaving the bathroom. I silently dry myself off and wrap the towel around my naked body.

I don't necessarily want to go back into the bedroom, but I can't exactly sleep in the bathroom. I take a few deep breaths and walk into the room. He's pulled his jeans and shoes back on, and when he looks over at me and the questions that I'm sure are written all over my face, he just shakes his head.

"Mad," I start with, having no clue where I'm going with the conversation.

"I'm hanging by a thread here, Em. Let's get one thing straight. It's never been that I don't want you. I just can't have you. Now, we're going to go back to bed and, in the morning, go get whatever shit you need from that piece-of-shit hotel you've been holed up in. We will NOT be going back to Syn. I'll have one of the guys come down with me to get your car. Don't look at me like that, Emmy. I won't bend on this. You aren't ready to go home—that's fucking fine. We'll go somewhere else and get that pretty little head of yours together. When you're ready, we go home. Simple as that."

"It isn't that simple, Maddox." I'm fuming. Who the hell does he think he is *telling* me what is going to happen with my life?

And just as soon as the last thought passes through my mind, I want to laugh. He's Maddox freaking Locke. Of course he is going to lay it out there in some unyielding demand. He's standing there, his naked chest and its sprinkling of dark hair making my hands twitch with the memory of what his skin feels like under my palms.

I cock my brow and invite him to continue.

He mirrors my move and crosses his tattooed arms over his massive chest.

Not to be outdone, I mimic his move. His brow rises, but he doesn't speak.

We're at an impasse. I'm not willing to be told what is going to happen in my life. And he isn't willing to let me run.

Little does he know, I'm the only one in control of *my* life. A life he made clear for years that he has no interest in sharing with me.

# CHAPTER 9
## Maddox

SHE'S SO damn beautiful when she's pissed. How have I never noticed just how appealing her ire is? I've seen just about every emotion possible from her over the years, but never has her anger been wholly turned on me.

"Get in the bed, babe."

She shakes her head, and if I weren't trying to teach her a lesson I would pull her over my knees and make her ass shine with my palm.

"Bed, Emmy."

Another shake, her honey-wheat eyes just begging for a fight.

"Emersyn," I warn.

"Maddox," she taunts.

Son. Of. A. Bitch.

Two strides are all it takes before I reach her. She takes a hasty step back, struggling with her footing, and in the middle of righting herself, her towel drops to the floor. My leg is throbbing since I hastily put my prosthetic back on to check on her, but I'll be fucking damned if I back down now. When I pull her towards me, her soft, naked body collides with my hard one. The noise that comes out of me is a mixture of a groan and a grunt. The feeling of her body in my arms is all it takes for me to push back the pain and take what is mine.

"I hate you," she whimpers weakly against my lips.

"You fucking love me, woman," I declare before crashing my mouth to hers and giving her a bruising kiss.

Her back hits the wall and her legs wrap around my waist. Careful to avoid her hips, my hands go to her ass and my fingers dig into her firm globes. I pull her towards my body so that there isn't any space between us. Her hands cup my cheeks and she manipulates my head so that she can devour my mouth, kissing me with everything she has.

Her hands move down my neck, kneading my pectorals and tweaking my nipples. I give her a few inches of space so that I can enjoy the feeling of her soft fingers and sharp nails scraping and rolling over my muscles. Every pass she makes has my skin burning in a painful pleasure.

Not once does our kiss break. She rubs against my throbbing dick, searching for her release. I might be a sorry bastard, but there isn't anything that can pull me away from her now. Not now that I know what it feels like to be between her thighs.

"Please don't stop this time," she begs against my mouth.

Not understanding her, I push through and thrust my hips into hers. She whimpers, and that sound is my undoing. I make sure I have my balance on my good leg before I remove one of my hands from the heaven of her ass and bring it to my jeans. I make quick work of the button, and in seconds, my cock is free to rub against her core. Kissing down her neck, I feel her slick wetness coating me. She moans when the thick head of my cock butts against her clit, and I lift my head to watch with fascination when she feels it.

Her eyes go wide, the fire behind them burning even brighter. When she leans back, her gaze travels down to where her pussy is hugging my weeping cock. She can't see everything, but she can see the silver loop through the head of my cock. I have three more running along the top of my shaft, but she'll feel those soon enough.

"Are you going to listen to me, Emersyn?" I inquire.

"In your dreams, Maddox," she spits back at me.

Then I smile when her eyes roll back in her head with one thrust of my hips. If she is this responsive with just my cock rubbing against her clit, I can't wait to see her come apart in my arms.

"If you think you're in control right now, angel, you're in for a wake-up call."

Her eyes narrow and I lean back, taking my cock in my free hand. Her expression flickers for a second, some of the desire clearing and a look of panic taking its place.

"Condom, Maddox." Her tone leaves no room for argument.

"I'm clean, Emmy," I say before leaning forward and kissing her collarbone. I rub my cock's head against her clit, coating it with her wetness and rolling my rigid flesh against her.

"But…after… Just please. You have to use one, Maddox."

I pull back and look into her eyes—the shame clear as day—and it kills me to know what she's gone through since she left.

"Okay, angel."

Her eyes get some of that heat back in them when I mumble the endearment. God, if she only knew.

I look to her left, thanking everything there is that, when I pushed her against the wall, we happened to be right next to the dresser, where I placed my wallet earlier. With one hand, still fighting to keep my balance and all of our weight on my good leg, I reach over and all but dump the entire contents on the wooden surface before I pull one of the gold packets and tear it open with my teeth. Her breathing is coming rapidly and her creamy skin is flushed with her arousal.

I lean back and push her into the wall with my thighs, giving me enough room to roll the latex on and also taking some of her off-centered weight off my legs. When the condom is in place, I rearrange our position so I have my hands back on her luscious ass and my cock primed and ready to pound into her wet heat. Our lips meet again, this time in a slow dance that isn't any less bruising than the previous kiss was. Without breaking our connection, I shift our lower bodies and push myself into her welcoming body. Inch by delicious inch.

Her head snaps back when she feels the first piercing in my ladder enter her body, her eyes wild and wide. When the second one pushes into her, her jaw drops. And as the last one joins the fun, she drops her head hard against the wall and purrs deep in her throat, the sound like a match to a gasoline-drenched timber. I'm burning to take her how I've been craving.

To control her body.

To claim her soul.

To make her mine.

I push the rest of the way into her tight cunt in one swift pass. The scream of pleasure that shoots out of her mouth echoes around the room, her slick walls clamping down on my cock. I groan when I feel her wetness coating my balls, and I can only hope that I last more than a few seconds.

Our coming together isn't all hearts and flowers. It's rough and raw. I slam into her with a force that makes the framed artwork hanging on the wall on top of the dresser shake against the wall.

The loud cries of her pleasure mix with my grunts and her begging dances with my praising.

It's fucking beautiful.

I don't waste my words when they aren't needed. I tell her everything I wish I could voice with my body. Her nails push into my shoulders with a sharp jab, and I use my hands on her ass to pull her roughly onto my cock. My leg is making it harder to take her as powerfully as I wish I could right now. The next time I take her, I'll have her ride me until she comes all over me.

"Oh, God! Oh, fuck. Yes! I'm going to come, Mad!" she screams while her pussy convulses against my shaft so forcefully that I falter in my glide out of her body. More wetness seeps from her core and roll down my thighs—proof of what *I* did to her.

Her body starts to go limp in my arms, and with a few more thrusts, I submerge my cock as deep as I can into her body and come so violently that my knees buckle. Not once in my awkward fall to my ass do I let go of her body.

I've had a slice of heaven and it's going to kill me to give it up.

# CHAPTER 10
## Emmy

IT TAKES my mind a lot longer than I care to admit to come back to Earth. Sex with Maddox is everything I thought it would be. All those times I rolled my eyes when reading a book and the heroine would claim that the Earth moved suddenly make sense. I don't think I've ever felt pleasure as intense as that in my life. Well, obviously, considering I've only had one other sexual partner in my life.

I shudder when I think of Shawn, and Maddox's arms tighten around me. He doesn't belong here. I know it seems like I should be upset or at the very least traumatized from what Shawn did to me, but I've promised myself to move forward. To not let him take anything else from me. And with Maddox's hands on my body, every thing else just falls away. It just feels *right.*

"Cold, Em?"

I give him a halfhearted grunt no and snuggle deeper into his chest. The short hairs under my face tickle and I smile. When his arms tighten again, I let out a contented sigh.

He holds me for a few minutes, his cock starting to soften inside me, and I moan with a weak protest when he slips from my body.

"Jump up, Em. Let me get this condom off and let's sleep. We have a lot we need to talk about tomorrow."

For once, I don't fight him on the issues that are still hanging over us. I'm not willing to give up this moment of peace between us. I have no illusions that this is some big 'ah ha' moment for us. Things between Maddox and me have never come easy, and just because we let the heat of the moment carry us this far doesn't in any stretch of the imagination mean he's going to profess his love for me.

I'm starting to think he just isn't wired to love. Either that or he just really doesn't feel the same way for me that I do for him.

I clean myself up and take a few seconds to clear my mind. If this night is all I get with him, then I'm going to ride the wave as long as I can. Morning is just a few short hours away and I don't want to waste a second I can spend in his arms.

He's standing against the wall when I open the door, his jeans still unbuttoned and the zipper down. Unfortunately, his cock isn't still out, because Lord knows I would love to get a good look at what I felt. I avoid his gaze and make my way into the room before climbing in bed. I listen to the sounds of him moving around in the bathroom and roll to my side, hoping that he doesn't push me away again when he comes back to bed.

The bathroom light shuts off, plunging the room into darkness, and I let my eyes drift shut as I listen to him remove his jeans before dropping on to the bed. When he doesn't immediately lie down, I let my worry start to fill my mind again. I listen as his boots hit the floor, one lightly and one with a heavy drop. I can hear his breathing, and it might as well be an echo of my heartbeat. It speeds up with each passing second, and I'm seconds away from crying.

This is it. He's going to reject me again.

I open my mouth to speak but snap it closed when he shifts his weight and drops down beside me. He doesn't take me in his arms like I hoped, and with a heavy exhale, I settle in with the knowledge that what we just shared could be considered a mistake to him. And that thought is a killer.

He shifts his body, moving around as if he is unable to find the right position, and right when I've all but given up all hope, his strong arm reaches over before pulling me into his body. When his heat seeps into my chilled skin, I mentally cry out with relief.

"Em," he implores. I can't understand why he is saying my name with such a pleading tone. Almost like me, he can't really wrap his mind around what just happened. "Tell me why you made me grab a condom."

Well, that certainly wasn't what I was anticipating.

"You know why, Maddox." I pray that he doesn't make me say it.

"Are you worried about it?" His fingers draw lazy circles against my shoulder as I think of the best way to express some of my darkest fears.

"You really know how to kill the moment, huh?" My joke falls flat and he remains silent—giving me the time I need to get out what needs to be said. "When Coop found me, before he brought me out to California, it was bad—real bad. The first thing I did was go to the doctor and get tested to make sure he hadn't given me something. You don't exactly expect your rapist to be exclusive to you. The tests all came back clean and I haven't been with anyone else. Until two weeks ago, when I went back to Syn. He hasn't touched me in almost two weeks and he wasn't there tonight, so he wouldn't have gotten to me then. But I won't lie to you. He didn't use protection the one time he took liberty with my body. So I would be lying if I said I wasn't worried."

He doesn't respond, but his fingers don't stop their caress against my skin.

"I wouldn't be able to live with myself if… I just couldn't take that chance. Not with you."

His arm tightens with my whispered words, and I close my eyes.

"There are things about me, things that I would rather you hear from my mouth before you see them for yourself. Things that I feel like you should know. I just don't know how to put it all out there for you, Em."

His rare open moment of sharing leaves me speechless. I'm not sure what he wants from me in this moment. I've learned from the past that you don't push Maddox, and when he's ready to tell you something, he'll do it on his time.

The silence becomes almost too much as I wait for him to go on. His fingers keep tracing imaginary lines on my skin. I shift my thoughts and try to picture what, if anything, he is drawing.

"I'm glad that Coop got you out of there. That he brought you into our lives. My life. Regardless of what happens tomorrow, you need to know that having you around for the last four years has meant more to me than you know."

I let out a gruff snort. "You have a funny way of showing that."

"Yeah."

"Mad—"

"Just give me a second to get it out, okay?" He cuts me off and

I snap my lips closed. "There is so much about me that you don't know, Em. I know that you feel like it would be easy for me to just let you all the way in, but I've spent my life learning to keep everyone out. I've watched every single person I've cared about suffer at my hands, and I can't live with the knowledge that you will be next. You're the angel that my demons beg to make fall. The pureness and light that my darkness wants to extinguish."

My heart breaks with each word muttered from of his lips.

"If I were a simple man, this would be so easy. Bottom line, Emmy, you deserve more than someone broken with more baggage than he can carry. You deserve the whole world and not just the smallest island on it."

I can't speak past the lump in my throat. A million thoughts rush through my mind. How he could ever think he's all of those things is beyond me. Why can't he see himself how everyone else around him does?

"Go to sleep, angel. We can talk in the morning, but tonight, just let me hold you." His fingers still and his large hand curls around my shoulder, pulling me deeper into his embrace.

I bring my legs up and tuck into his side, slowly dragging my arm over his thick muscles before resting my hand against his warm chest. If this really is the only moment I'll ever have with him, then I'm going to commit each second to memory so that I can remember it when I go back to my life as the Princess of Syn.

Right before I nod off, I throw out the only lifeline I have left. "We all have baggage, Maddox. I wish that you could understand that I'm not asking for perfection. What you fail to realize is that I have two arms just begging for you to let me help you carry that baggage."

His arm tightens almost painfully and his body goes solid. It takes him a minute of loud inhalations before his body relaxes again.

"Goodnight, Emmy."

"Goodnight, Maddox."

# CHAPTER 11
## Emmy

"I SWEAR TO Christ, Asher, if you lost her again, I'm going to kick your fucking ass. Yeah, I get that you have things going on. No. I'll be home in a few days and you better have my shit in order and her sitting like a queen on my couch."

My eyes snap open and I zero my stare in on where he's standing and looking out the window. Who the hell is he talking about?

"Don't give me that shit, Asher. Yeah, what the fuck ever." He's silent as he listens to whatever Asher is saying to him, and after a few more clipped responses, he ends the call and tosses his phone on the desk. Turning his face gives nothing away when he realizes that I've been watching him.

I shake my head when I realize that this is how he's going to play it. We're back to stupid Emmy and silent Maddox.

After throwing back the sheet, I move to stand in front of him. His eyes flash for the briefest of moments before he schools his expression. Well, at least we know he isn't indifferent to my nude body.

"What am I supposed to wear?" I ask in a tone that oozes sarcasm.

He doesn't speak. Instead, he moves around my body and grabs a bag off the floor behind me. Then he holds it out to me. I keep looking into his eyes, watching the deep, dark brown remain expression and emotionless.

"Right. When you're ready to use your big-boy words, maybe we can continue this playdate."

I reach up to take the bag, but before my fingertips can wrap around the strap, he lets it fall to the floor. I watch it fall, taking my eyes off him, and before I can rip him a new one, I'm pressed against his clothed body and his lips are dueling with mine. After kissing the wind out of my sails, he releases me, bends, grabs the bag, and once again holds it in my direction.

I snatch the bag from him and stomp into the bathroom, childishly slamming the door behind me—just because I can.

Once I throw my long hair into a messy bun, I open the bag to find my own clothes. My brow creases as I try to come up with a logical reason to explain why he would have my own things—things I know I didn't pack when I left town. I quickly get dressed, throwing on a pair of yoga pants and T-shirt. When I exit the room, he is still standing by the window, his hands pushed into his pockets and his posture almost relaxed—something that is rarely seen with him.

"How did you get my clothes?"

"Grabbed them when I got Cat." He doesn't turn, so I have to quickly turn my shocked expression into some verbal response to that news.

"And why did you have Cat?"

"Because you ran. Someone needed to take care of her."

"Yeah? That someone was Melissa. Cohen was going to

babysit for a while," I snap back. I'm primed for a fight now.

"Don't make me kiss that sass right out of your mouth, Emersyn. A lot happens when you're gone for a little over a month. Melissa had an accident. Everyone is okay now, but for a while, there was a lot of unknown. Part of the reason it took me so long to get to you was because I needed to go back home and help out while Greg was at the hospital with Melissa and the twins."

His words take my fight and squash it. Just like that, he knocks me down a few pegs. Melissa, out of all the girls, I connected the most with. Our friendship is one of the many things I've missed since I ran. I called her after I left my letter with Axel to ask her to grab my cat, but I've been so busy living in my own head that I haven't even called her since.

"She okay? The girls?" I beseech, desperate to know that they're okay.

"They're fine now. You need to call her. She's worried about you—they all are."

I can't respond to him. My mind is racing at just how much I have let the people who have come to be my family down. Very briefly, the thought crosses my mind that, if Coop hadn't run into me all those years ago, their lives would be so much better, but I quickly dismiss it. There is a reason for everything, and as unjust as it is, he was meant to come into my life—even if it was the beginning of the end for him.

"What are you thinking?" Maddox asks, letting his stoic exterior slip. His head is cocked slightly, his brows furrowed and his lips pursing. He has no idea how attractive he is either, which just adds to his appeal.

"How better off they would have been if Coop had never found me."

"Excuse me?" His tone is hard and unforgiving.

"Don't make me repeat myself. I'm not fishing here, but repeating what I was thinking. Things would be so different if that day hadn't happened."

"Yeah, you're damn fucking right it would be."

"I don't know why you're getting so pissed, Mad. I thought it. I can't exactly *control* my fleeting thoughts. I was the one he took that bullet for. Take me out of the equation and what do you get? You get Coop. THAT is what you get."

He shakes his head and moves to pull me closer, but I step away from him. His nostrils flare and his jaw twitches, but he doesn't say anything.

"You really believe that, don't you?"

I nod my head and he drops his. I watch as he runs his hand over his scalp and clasps the back of his neck. I can hear him muttering to himself but can't make out his words.

"Let me explain something to you. If you hadn't have been there, there would have been a handful of different situations. One, he would have stepped in front of Dee. Two, he would have been late walking in and Dee would have been there alone. We could have had anyone sitting in your desk and it wouldn't have mattered to Coop. He would have jumped in front of that gun regardless of who the intended target was. That's just who he was, and I know deep fucking down you know I'm right. Stop thinking about all the things that could have happened and be thankful that you're alive and knew him for the time you did." His chest is heaving when he finishes, and before I can open my mouth, he just holds his hand up and walks around me…straight out the door.

I know he's right. I've been using my anger with myself so I haven't had to feel all of the pain I felt right after he died. The pain of losing someone so dear to me. There isn't a fear I've known in my life like looking into the barrel of a gun-wielding maniac. I think a small part of myself will always feel somewhat responsible for his death *because* of the fact that he died saving me. Bottom line, Maddox is right. I should be focusing on the fact that I even knew him—regardless of how long that period was.

*"Chin up, buttercup."* Oh, the irony.

With no idea where I am or what I'm supposed to do if he doesn't come back, I settle into the bed and flip on the television. I focus on the program, something about grown woman acting like some hilarious rip-off of Toddlers and Tiaras. I watch but allow my mind to wander. I can't believe that I've been gone for almost five weeks and I haven't even thought about checking in. What kind of friend doesn't even give a thought to those left behind?

Maybe Maddox is right. Maybe I should go back. But how do I do that when I'm not sure I can even let go of this guilt? I can't go back until I know with no doubt that I'm fixed. It's time to pick up the pieces of my life and stop living in the fear of the unknown.

MADDOX COMES back an hour later. His mood is much better and his arms are full of food. We sit in a somewhat comfortable silence while we eat. For him, that's normal, but I'm still trying to figure out if I'm willing to go back—or if I should go back to

Syn, where I've always felt like I would end up rotting away in my destined role of the princess.

"Are you done thinking all that bullshit?" he asks between mouthfuls of his burger.

"Depends on which bullshit you're referring to."

"Don't play games, Em. Do you still think that we're better off having never met you? That I'm better off?"

"I don't know how to answer that, okay? I want to believe that I'm just speaking out of my ass, but I can't help how I feel. I'm working on it, and honestly, Maddox, that's the best I can give you right now."

He drops his burger and nods his head. "I used to think the same thing. Had I done something—anything—different that my life would have taken a different path. I used to think that maybe there was one thing that could have stopped the snowball from going out of control."

"And what changed?"

"You did." He drops my eyes and starts to clean his mess up. "Are you done?" He doesn't wait for me to actually respond but continues to clean up around me.

"How the hell did I change your way of thinking?"

"No matter what I did to make you hate me, you still came back for more. You were unbiased with your feelings towards anything I threw at you."

"You're making no sense, Maddox." My mind is swirling with everything he's saying. I just have no idea what to make of it all.

"Nothing, Em. Just forget I said anything."

"I can't just forget that! You don't sit here and say all of that to me and just say, 'Oops, just kidding! Forget I finally opened my mouth!'" I stand back from my seat at the desk and march into his space, taking the trash and throwing it on the floor. "What did I ever do to make you hate me so much?"

"What does it matter? I used to think that I could have changed my future. I used to think that I could manipulate those around me into *not* caring so that, in return, I didn't harm them. And then you came into my life and there was no changing you. So, yeah, Emmy… I used to think that I could have changed my path in life, but now, I know that I've just been playing the game of fate and there isn't shit I can do to make it any better. I am what I am, and all that is *me* will do nothing but pull you under a riptide you'll never survive."

"I don't even know what to say to that."

"So don't say anything," he says with sadness.

"I wish you could see yourself how I see you. Or maybe if you would let me in, open up to me, I would understand a little better why you continue to break my heart. At this point, Mad, I'm not sure I'll ever be able to put it back together again."

His eyes darken and his lips part when he sucks in a deep breath.

He steps out shortly after to make some calls. I don't ask. I just curl up into the covers and pray that sleep takes me away from the harshness of reality.

# CHAPTER 12
## *Maddox*

ONE NIGHT. I spend one night between her thighs and suddenly my walls are crumbling down. Mentally, I'm frantically trying to repair their damage. Attempting to reinforce them against the tempting allure of her love. It would be so easy to fall at her feet and beg her for everything she's ever offered me. I want to; God, I want to. But right now, what's important is getting her the hell out of here and doing what I need to do to fix whatever is going on in her pretty head. I have no doubt that she is suffering greatly at his loss, but now, after hearing how she grew up, I fear that her issues might go deeper.

Regardless of what is going on around us, I feel unsettled with the hope that's building within. The hope that maybe, just maybe, it's okay to let her in. I don't know what to do with that feeling. I've spent so long refusing to believe in it that it's terrifying.

I woke up before the sun and started making plans and getting the ball rolling. I rented us a place about an hour from home—a cabin that one of our contacts owns. He is going to be overseas for the next couple of months and needs someone to keep an eye on his place. In reality, I could have just as easily passed this job to someone more local to him, but this is just what Emmy needs.

Somewhere neutral. Not back home, where our friends care too much to give her the time she needs, and damn sure not in this hellhole I found her in.

I take a moment after returning to our room to watch her sleep. She doesn't look sad when she's sleeping. I hate the part I've played in her sadness. This time away—together—will be good for us. If I really am going to forget everything that's been integrated into my life since birth, then I need to make sure she can handle this baggage she is so willing to help me carry.

If there really is a future with us, then this is the time to find out.

Letting her sleep, I go about cleaning up the mess in the room and carry the few belongings we had with us down to my Charger before settling into the chair in the corner and watching my angel. I sit there in the shadows of the room and let myself *feel*, something I rarely do and never do when someone can see me. I let the future that could be us play out in my mind, feeling that flicker of hope grow a little larger when I can't see anything but her love for me… and mine for her.

WE'VE BEEN on the road for a few hours now and she remains silent. I know she's still fuming that I followed through with my promise that she wouldn't be going back to Syn. We went by her hotel room, and as she stood pissed in the middle of the room, I packed her belongings into her suitcases. Five minutes later, we were back in the car and on our way to Georgia.

I keep my mouth shut. There really isn't anything for me to gain by allowing her to pick a fight. She wants to feel like she's in control of her life, and by me swooping in and taking over, she's free-falling. It's not that I'm trying to do that. I just want to make sure she's where she belongs and not dancing for a room full of assholes while being at the hands of that motherfucker… Now that is not where she belongs.

One day, maybe she will see where I'm coming from, but if I have to get nothing but her anger in return for her safety, then I'm okay with that.

"Where are we going, Mad?" she whispers hoarsely.

"Not home, so stop worrying about it. We're going to a cabin in Pine Hills. It's sitting on fifty acres in the middle of nowhere. You need time, I get that, but you also need help getting over everything. So when you're ready, we go home—but not until you're ready."

She's quiet for so long that I look over at her. Her mouth is hanging slack, her eyes bugged out in shock.

"*I* need time? *I* need to get over everything? Well, isn't that magnanimous of you, Maddox Locke." She laughs, the sound hitting my ears and making me cringe. "Maybe while we're there, we can find a mirror for you to look in and repeat that shit you just shoveled at my feet to yourself. Hello? Pot, meet kettle."

"This isn't about me, Emmy."

"Oh, you stupid, stupid man. It's *always* been about you."

I don't let her see it, but her words hit home. She couldn't have delivered a more direct shot if she'd tried. Sure, she doesn't know what she just did. *She doesn't know because you never let her in, you idiot.* My mother's words come back to me like a tsunami. The pain of always being her stupid little boy tries to take root, but I brush it aside. Emmy is nothing like my mother, and even as careless as her words are, she's talking out her hurt right now.

"Emersyn," I start. "Don't let my desire to protect you be confused as stupidity. It has never been about me. I don't keep myself from you because I think it's some fun goddamn game." I pause, needing a second to swallow the lump in my throat. I'm trying so hard to keep my heart from breaking free from my body. The emotions I've hidden for so long are rattling the cages, just waiting for that moment to pounce, and it terrifies me to think of what will be left of me if they get out. "I've been told my whole life that I was the worst kinds of evil. That my soul is as black as my eyes and that everything and everyone I touch will wilt at my hands. So, Emmy, *this,*" I stress, pointing between us, "THIS has never, not once, been about me."

The rest of the ride is uncomfortable at best. I never intended to tell her that much. I struggle during every mile with what I could say to take that verbal vomit and shovel it back in. She knows more with just those few sentences than anyone else in my life.

And I'm terrified to think about what she must think of me now. The man she has loved unconditionally for years isn't who she thinks he is. I'm sure she regrets every second of it now. I'm not sure what unsettles me more—the thought that she might regret giving her love or that she might be afraid of the truth of me.

Or worse…that she'll take that love away and never give it back.

# LOCKE

WHEN WE get to Devon's cabin, I leave her to her exploring. She retreats to one of the back bedrooms and shuts the door softly behind her. I give her that play, knowing that she's processing my words.

I make sure that everything is stocked and we'll be set for the unforeseeable future. When that's done, I'm left with nothing left to do. The television holds no appeal. I call and check in with Axel then settle on the couch. Knowing that I have some time alone, I take a second to rub the pained muscles in my thighs. I need to get my prosthetic off before I do more damage than necessary to my stump. It's been a long few weeks and I've felt like this was coming for a while now. Usually when the skin gets too irritated for me to wear the prosthetic, I work from home, giving the skin the rest it needs and, sometimes, the sores time to heal. Keeping my weight off it for a while does the trick but never fixes the issue.

I've come to live with this part of my future. I hate every moment of it, but it's my reality.

"What's wrong with your leg?"

Her question startles me. I was so lost in my own head that I didn't even hear her coming into the room.

I immediately pull my hand off my leg. "Nothing."

"Is that how this is going to be now? Okay. Why don't I tell you what *I* think is wrong with your leg? I think this might be a little more forthcoming than waiting for you to snap the hell out of it and admit that I'm standing right in front of you, wanting to help carry your fucking burdens."

I narrow my eyes and do my best to tell her to shut the hell up without words. The feeling of helplessness, an emotion I haven't felt in years, floods my system.

"Nothing to say, Maddox? Not that I should be surprised."

"Emersyn, shut your mouth."

"No!" she screams. "I will not *shut my mouth*! I'm sick of *shutting my mouth.* Guess what, big boy? This poor little naïve girl sees you. I see through the bullshit you put up as a shield. I see through the anger you push on others to keep them at arm's length. I see past it all. The pain that is deep within you. The shame, fear, and helplessness. I see you!" She finishes, screaming her words at me with so much force that her skin is flushed and her breathing is accelerated. "I see *you*," she whispers. "All of you."

"You have no idea what you're talking about." I dismiss her wrath and try to ignore the shitstorm that's coming, hoping she gives it up and goes back to the room.

"I know exactly what I'm talking about. I know because my soul recognizes its mate. Its kindred spirit. We both have our pain, Maddox. We both have the shame of our past and the fear it holds on the future. The only difference is you let that pain and fear rule your heart. And the difference in me is that I am willing to risk it all day in and day out for just a second of your love."

She's right. I couldn't have said it better myself.

"Tell me why you were massaging your leg, Maddox," she implores.

I can tell by her tone that she knows. I have no idea how since I've been very careful over the years to keep my…disability…hidden from everyone but the guys.

"How do you know?" I sigh.

"Tell. Me. What is wrong, Maddox." She lifts her arms and plants her hands on her hips. Her stance is screaming that she is unwilling to fold. She won't give this up until she gets whatever she is after.

"Stop pressing this, Em!" I bellow, my voice loud enough to shake the windows in their frames.

"What is bothering your leg, Mad?!" she yells back, just as pissed with me as I am with her for not giving this up.

"Fuck!" I shout. I don't take my eyes off hers as I jerk my jeans up, yank my stocking down, and remove my leg. I replace the shame I feel for having her see my crippled body with anger. With my prosthetic in my hand, I toss it in her direction and hold her eyes as it lands right next to her feet. "Is that what you wanted, Emersyn? You want to see just how broken I am? It isn't enough to know that my fucking head is a mess. You want to see just how badly my body is ruined too?"

We hold each other's glare—both unwilling to be the first one to break. The rage bubbling inside me is becoming too much to bear. With a roar, I lean forward and flip the coffee table over. The books, so perfectly placed on its surface, go flying, and right before the table crashes with a loud boom through the still cabin, I lose my balance. The force I used to push forward on the couch and the momentum of my rage sends me falling right behind it to the floor.

She doesn't even flinch. Her stance doesn't change and her ice-cold fury never leaves its hold on my eyes.

"Do you feel better now?" she grinds out. "Does it feel better to throw things and act like a child? Maybe while you're down there, you can kick and scream and beg me for a toy before we leave the store next time? Hmm?"

"Shut up, Emersyn." My weak voice lacks conviction as I let the humiliation and shame of her seeing me like this fall over me.

"I'm not going to shut up! How can you be so foolish? You want to know how long I've known you're an amputee? Three years. For three years, I've known, and even through it all, I never let it change how I saw you. I never told anyone because that isn't my place, but I'll tell you this much, Maddox. Your pride is misplaced in this situation. I don't look at you and see someone *broken*," she says, echoing my earlier self-loathing like a smack in the face before delivering home her final blow. "I have admired you for everything you've overcome and continue to overcome. I see you as perfect, and in my eyes, this makes you honorable, brave, and heroic. It doesn't lessen you as a person. It's just another one of the things I've loved about you since the very beginning."

She leaves me on the floor. My leg is still lying carelessly a few feet away, where I threw it in the middle of my tantrum.

The shock of her words hits my system and my breath stills in my throat. The power behind each word she just put out there smacks into my chest and shakes me to my very core.

All the while, that fucking flame of hope gets a little brighter.

# CHAPTER 13
## Emmy

BETWEEN THE bullshit he's convinced makes him unworthy of my heart, the desire that is even larger now that we know what it feels like to allow it to break free, and the personal battles we're both dealing with, the last week has been tense at best.

I know enough from the bits and pieces he's told me that his hurt runs deep. Probably even deeper any one person should ever feel to get to that level of self-hatred. Until he lets me in, there really isn't anything I can do about it though, so I leave him to his thoughts and try to keep the distance from making me bitter.

We co-exist. He's kept himself closed off and I've been working towards forgiving myself for the events that led up to Coop's death. I know now that I was letting my grief over losing him take hold. I shouldn't have run from my life just because of the things I was feeling. Even if I hadn't frozen at that moment, someone still would have been hurt. It will never take the pain away from losing him, but I no longer blame myself. He wanted me to live. He will always hold a special place in my heart and I'll do my best to live by his motto—after all, you only live once.

I laugh as I think about all the times he would scream, "YOLO!"

at the top of his lungs. It didn't matter where we were, he was going to do what made him happy and live for the moment—something I've vowed to do myself over the last week.

"What's so funny?" Maddox grumbles when I walk past him. He has taken it upon himself to get up at the ass crack of dawn the last few days and have breakfast ready by the time I roll out of bed. It's one of the rare times he allows himself to be in the same room I'm in.

"Just thinking about Coop," I reply with a smile. "His outlook on life and how I'm going to do better to honor his memory by living life like him."

I jump when the pan he was cleaning slams down against the marble countertop. Turning from where I was fixing my plate, I find him standing just a breath from me. Close enough that it wouldn't take much for me to take his thick bottom lip and give him a smart bite.

"What the fuck?" he fumes.

"What the fuck what?" I snap back with confusion. I cock my head and wait for him to elaborate over his newest tantrum. My mind is still thinking about those lips, so it takes me a second too late to catch where he's going with this.

"So you're just going to spread those legs for anyone that walks by? Become what? A little whore?"

"Excuse me?" I gasp.

"Coop believed in one thing and that was having a good time." His eyes go from dark brown to black in seconds.

I watch the stages of pure rage take over his features, and even though I'm becoming more pissed by the each passing moment of his silent, irate bullshit, I can't help but think how perfectly handsome he looks when he's angry.

"One thing he lived for was pussy. He didn't give a fuck about where it came from as long as it ended up riding his dick. So let me clarify—you will not become a slut like Coop was."

My hand moves without permission, clapping against his cheek and leaving not only an instant red mark, but also needle pricks shooting up my arm.

"How fucking dare you speak about him that way. Do not let your misplaced anger turn his memory to shit. I woke up this morning determined to be happy—to live in the moment. And right now, in this moment, I want to kick your fucking ass. YOLO, you jerk."

I take deep pulls of oxygen, trying desperately to tame the fire that wants to consume my body. I've never been a violent person, but right now, all I can see is red.

His head is still turned to the side; the bright red mark against his tan skin taunts me. When his head slowly and methodically turns back to glare at me, I give him back as good as he gives.

I've seen him mad before. Hell, he's Maddox Locke; he's mad ninety percent of the time. But this—this rage directed towards me—is something I have never witnessed before. Knowing that he would never hurt me physically helps me stand strong and hold my own. He deserved that and I'm not backing the hell down.

Expecting a verbal lashing, I'm surprised when his rough hands grab my head and pull me towards him. My gasp works in his favor, and in just seconds, we're tearing the clothes from each other's bodies. Our anger fuels the desire—the craving for each other. Our teeth clash as we fight for dominance with our lips. His hands finish pulling my shorts from my body and then lift my hands from his belt before bringing them behind my back. In one second, I go from battling for control to giving it up completely.

With his large hand holding my wrists together behind my back, he pulls back for a second to look me in the eyes. His anger hasn't dissipated in the least. His eyes are pitch black and his skin is even more flushed than it was before. My handprint still bright against his cheek reminds me just what set this in motion.

"I hate you," I snap, for the first time wishing that I were capable of even an ounce of hate. Then it would be so much easier to move on.

He lets my wrists go, but my freedom is short-lived. He grabs me around the waist and flips my position. My bare chest hits the cold, unbending counter. My panties are ripped from my body in one swift snap. Then he reaches back up with his hands and grabs my arms, pulling until he has my wrists once again hostage at the small of my back.

"Tell me," he demands.

"I hate you," I parrot weakly.

The smack of his palm against my ass takes me by surprise. Not because of the pain—it does hurt in an oddly pleasurable way—but because I never thought he would really spank me.

"Give me the words, Emersyn."

I hardly recognize his voice at this point. I'm so turned on that my head is spinning. I can feel my wetness running down my thighs.

Apparently, I didn't speak quickly enough, because his palm comes back down lower on my ass. The shot of pleasure that zips from that one heated mark goes straight to my core and I'm convinced that one more of those strong smacks and I'll come on the spot.

"Give. Me. The. Words." He drives each word home with another smaller smack, each time making sure he doesn't hit the same spot twice.

"I want to hate you," I whisper. At this point, I'm not sure why I'm egging him on.

"You fucking love me, woman!" he bellows.

Then he brings his hand down, this time harder than each of the previous times. He doesn't even pause before rolling his hand over the offended skin and plunging two fingers deep within my waiting body.

"Oh, God!" I cry.

My walls clamp down instantly and my whole body shakes with the power behind my impending orgasm. My muscles are seizing, coiling tight, and preparing for the force that will flood my system soon. I'm right there, standing on the ledge and ready to jump…and then he pulls his fingers from my body.

"What the hell!" I screech.

"Shut up!" he thunders.

"Don't tell me to shut up!" I shout back, working to free my arms from his unbreakable hold. "Let me go, asshole." I want to cry at the loss of what promised to be such an all-consuming release.

When he shifts, I feel the blunt head of his cock at my entrance.

"Condom!" I yell through the hunger I feel towards this man.

"Shut up," he pants.

"Don't tell me—"

My words are cut off when he pushes himself roughly into my body. I yelp out when I feel him bottom out, and as he rolls his hips, I feel every single one of his delicious piercings.

Everything else around us falls to the wayside. He takes my body forcefully and I take everything he's giving me just as hard, meeting him thrust for thrust. My hands itch to break free, to try to take the control he so clearly desires in this moment.

"Give me the words, Em." His grunted command breaks through the silence that only our harsh breaths were filling just moments before.

"Fuck you!" I shout when he slams into my body.

"You are," he laughs.

If I weren't so close to flying into a million pieces, I might find it insulting that he's laughing at me. At the moment, though, the only thing I can think about is every inch of his cock buried deep within my body.

"Now, Emersyn."

I smile to myself, knowing that he can't see my face, and refuse to give him the words he wants. I screech when his palm connects with my ass again, my wetness coating his cock and my orgasm just within reach.

And then he stops. His hips still and he just stands there with his cock twitching inside my body.

"What the hell are you doing?! Fuck me, Maddox!"

"Not until you give me the words I want, Em."

He lets my wrists go and curls his fingers around my waist, lifting me up from the counter so that my feet can no longer touch the floor. Then he rolls his hips and I roll my eyes.

"Tell me," he commands.

"I love you! I fucking love you. Are you happy now?" I lift up on the counter and turn my head to glare at him.

My mind instantly stills when I see the completely open expression of happiness on his face. His cheeks are still flushed, his eyes are boring into mine, and his mouth is tipped up in a smile so shocking that my breath catches.

"Yeah, angel, I am."

He pulls out slowly, his eyes never leaving mine, before pushing back in. He holds my gaze—his smile more of a smirk now—and gradually builds me back up. It doesn't take long before his thrusts are coming quicker and his veins are throbbing in his neck. I throw my head back and scream loud and long when he hits that perfect spot deep inside me that has me coming hard against his dick. He gives me a few good thrusts before he comes on a roar.

His fingers move from my hips and caress my back on a lazy trail up my spine. When he hits my shoulders, his hand curls in and pulls me up until my back is flush with his chest. The light spattering of hair there sends a violent shiver through my body. I feel his groan rumble against my back at my slight movement. His free hand comes up, cups my jaw, and turns my head so that our lips are just a breath away.

Holding my eyes hostage, he gives me a short kiss before pulling back. "I'm sorry," he whispers. When he pulls out of my body, his fingers once again fall down my spine as he walks out of the kitchen.

Leaving me to wonder what in the hell just happened.

# CHAPTER 14
## Maddox

IT'S BEEN two days since we came together in anger.

I immediately gave her some weak-ass apology and kept my distance while I tried to figure out why I'd demanded her love. I don't even know what had come over me. I know how she feels. She's made no secret of it for the longest time. The words were on the tip of my tongue to return her love…but my fear kept me from speaking. So I took the space I needed to get my head together. That night—with some unspoken truce—I decided to give in and see what happens.

To let her in and the blessed promise that her love provides.

She asked me to teach her how to shoot, to help her learn how to handle firearms the night after our kitchen sex. She expressed the helplessness she felt when she didn't have the means to protect herself and that, if she were ever in that position again, she wanted to be prepared.

"I'll teach you, Em, but mark my words—you'll never be in a position like that again."

"You can't promise me that. You aren't going to be with me every second of my life," she deadpanned.

I heard what she wasn't saying. She was hesitant to believe that I'm trying. I don't blame her. Hell, I wouldn't trust me easily either.

"I damn sure can."

"All right, big boy. Let's not argue the semantics here. Will you teach me?"

"Yeah, babe. I'll teach you."

That afternoon was one of the best in my life. She was nervous at first, but she's a natural, so it didn't take long to get her on a roll. We joked with each other and enjoyed being in the moment. The heaviness that usually swallows us whole was absent, and even with knowing that we have no control over the unknown, there wasn't a thing that could ruin the day.

The following week, we spend our days in the backfield shooting the targets Devon has lined up. His collection of firearms is vast and Emmy never tires.

And our nights are spent getting lost in each other.

I WENT back to my apartment a week ago and got Cat for Emmy. My thoughts were that she would help Emmy want to go home. We've been here for a little over a month now, and even though I would probably be content spending the rest of my life in this weird bubble we've created, I know it's not fair to her. She deserves a life, and now that she's starting to become stronger as a person, I know it's time to talk about going home.

The one thing we've been avoiding is talking about my past. She's told me more about the hell she grew up in. I had to fight myself in wanting to drive back down to Florida and make some heads roll. I can't believe how strong she is, and she's told me over and over that it wouldn't change anything to go back.

One step forward. That's what she keeps telling me. I want to smile, to accept it and let my past go, but I have to wonder if, with each step forward, we aren't really taking ten back. And that is because I still haven't let her in completely.

*Tell her about your family!* My mind has been screaming the same thing over and over to me since that morning in the kitchen. And for the first time in years, I'm considering opening up the hell I grew up in and letting her see all of my broken soul. I've battled back and forth with whether just telling her could dampen some of the innocence she still has.

I let myself remember the night before and the nightmare that gave me the push I needed in the right direction. The direction that will take me away from her.

Once again, I was stuck back in the blast zone, pulling what should have been Morris—but it was Emmy. I was able to crawl back from that nightmare only to have a new one take its place. One that put Emmy in the reach of my family. In the dream, I saw her look at me with so much anger and pain because I had ruined her life. I can't even remember the words she was screaming—all I knew was that I had done that to her. And before I was able to pull myself out of the dream, I saw Emmy, my angel, dying at her own hands because she couldn't take the darkness in my soul.

"What's on your mind?" Emmy asks as she plops down on the couch with Cat in her arms. She lazily strokes her fur and waits for me to answer.

Her stunning smile makes my chest hurt. I give her a glance before looking back down at my iPad. I'm trying desperately to forget the images that were just in my mind. Trying to harden my heart over what I know will be the final blow to her love.

"There's some stuff going on back home that we need to get back for, Em."

"What kind of stuff?" she inquires. She didn't shoot it down, so that's a plus.

"Asher. He's been investigating the man who held the strings in Coop's murder. Without letting any of us in. He's in deep, babe. Deep enough that we need to decide how this plays out and quick."

"Holy shit," she whispers.

"Yeah, that about sums it up. They called a meeting and I need to be there. I would really like you to come back with me. You need to come home and let your friends love you."

"Let my friends love me?" she questions sarcastically.

"Yeah, Em."

"And what about you?"

"I can't give you that, Em. I'm not even sure I know how."

"You really, truly believe that, huh?" She laughs and lets Cat jump from her lap. Even the cat gives me a look of disgust.

"It isn't that I believe it without proof. It's all I've known, Em. The only thing that I know of love is that it isn't real."

She throws her head back and laughs. "It isn't real?"

I nod, and she gives me a cold smile.

"So Axel and Izzy? Greg and Melissa? I suppose Beck doesn't love Dee? You're right. They must really hate each other." When her eyes go cold, I feel my own narrow in return. "All of these people around you give you proof that love is real and you still sit there believing that bullshit you've convinced yourself of. You're the one who helped each and every one of them get together you still sit there refusing to believe in it. Refusing to believe in me… in us."

"Emer—"

"No. I don't want to hear it, Maddox. You want to go home—fine. I don't have a home there anymore, so if you're going to make me come with you, then it looks like you have a roommate until I can see about renting my apartment back." She stands and starts to storm from the room.

"Emersyn Rose, sit your fucking ass down now."

Her back gets stiff, but shockingly, she turns and marches back to the couch. Throwing herself down with a huff, she folds her arms under her perfect tits and waits to see what my next move is.

"You want to know why I keep you locked out? You want me to give you a little bit of the depressing life of Maddox Locke?"

Her eyes flash, but I press on. If she's determined to know it all, then I'll give it to her.

"I was born into old money. My mother fucked the pool boy, and nine months later, the child she called her demon seed baby was born. The evil mistake of her sins born to do nothing but destroy everything. I have never, not once in thirty-six years, had a nice comment from my mother. My earliest memory is of her telling me not to play with my brother because my black soul will taint him. Yeah, my own mother said I would taint him. The one time Mason fell off his bike, on his own accord, I spend a week not able to sit because she beat me. She blamed me for his accident just because I was near him. I'll spare you the rest of the details, but they aren't pretty, and it's been one big 'fuck you' after another until the last day I saw her."

I take a breath and have to look away from her. The tears of pity are not something I care to see.

"The last time I saw her was right after I woke up from the bombing that took my leg. She took great care in reminding me how fucked up I was. That the two men who had lost their lives that day were just another thing my black soul had ruined. That I had killed them because they'd had the misfortune of being around me that day. She then dug the knife deeper, telling me that my fiancée had been working with them to trick me into signing over my part of the Locke fortune."

I lay my head back and try not to let the memories of that day drag me under. "I think the final nail was when she told me the child I had thought my own was Mason's, my brother. So yeah, Em, I don't really think I know how to do love, and even if I let myself believe that what we have is strong enough to beat my demons, my black soul, I'm too scared that I'll drag you under in the process and you'll never recover."

I don't give her a second to respond. I climb slowly from the couch and toss my iPad down in the seat. "You can stay with me until you get on your feet again. We'll leave in the morning."

I walk out of the room and spend the rest of the evening in a nice rage-filled self-loathing pity party. When I'm finally able to drift off to sleep, I'm awoken what feels like minutes later covered in sweat, my throat raw from my screams.

I had the nightmare again that I was back in my past. Only this time when I sat in the hospital bed and listened to my mother lay into me, it was Emmy. My sweet Emmy was there, telling me how she will never forgive me for ruining her life.

# CHAPTER 15
## Emmy

WE'VE BEEN home for a few weeks now. At first, I wouldn't leave the apartment. Even though I had come to terms with the memories of being home and not seeing one of my best friends, it didn't mean that I was necessarily ready to move on. I missed him. However, it was getting easier to deal with each day.

One of the hardest parts of being back was my strained relationship with Maddox. We've hardly spoken to each other since that last day at the cabin. Chipped responses here and there and notes on the counter telling me that he wouldn't be home filled up the first week. I heard from one of the girls that he had been sleeping at the office while they finished up their dealings with Dominic Murphy. Things haven't been any easier since that.

Right when they let their guard down, Chelcie was put in harm's way again. I don't remember much from my standoff with Sarah Jane. It's almost as if I had been having an out-of-body experience. I can see the events of that day playing out, but I can't tell you how I knew what to do. Izzy told me that she thinks it was Coop who'd made sure they were safe. I hadn't planned on going to see Chelcie that day. I had planned on apartment hunting, but it was almost as if I'd *had* to give her her gift right that second. The rest was either just damn good luck or maybe Izzy is onto something.

I like to think that maybe it was a little of Coop watching out for us and making sure that his son was okay.

The night after the showdown with Sarah Jane was the worst. When the adrenaline crashed and I realized that I had actually shot another human, things were not pretty. I went from jazzed beyond belief to a sobbing mess curled into a ball in the shower.

Maddox blamed himself for having taught me how to use a gun and then again for having made it readily available. We fought and it ended in another rough crashing together of our bodies. This time, though, I was the one to get up from the floor and leave *him* with an "*I'm sorry.*" It isn't right. We keep coming together for a reason, but I've started to realize that I might never get to beat through his beliefs. I can't think of a way to make him *believe* in us. His mind keeps telling him no, to stay away and keep me out. But his heart—God, his beautiful heart—keeps calling out to me, and like a glutton for punishment, I keep going back for more.

I can't even explain where my mind is right now. I'm mad—that's a given—but I've also started to lose my faith. I've lost the way to my happiness and I'm not really sure how to get it back. I'm stuck in a rut, and honestly, I'm thinking it would be better if I just throw in the towel and leave. Not run, but go somewhere else and get my head on right. Somewhere where he isn't. I can't keep fighting for someone who refuses to consider my love for him. It's like beating a horse when he's already down. Every time he rejects me and my heart shatters more, I just know I won't recover from the pain if I stick around.

Tonight, we need to actually be social and not kill each other, so I told him that I am leaving. We fought all day today, and this time, it didn't even end in a rough coupling. This time when I screamed in his face that I hated him, I almost believed it—and I could tell by the look that flashed across his face that he did too. And that terrified me.

It was the first time he didn't demand I 'give him the words.'

So now here we are, on the way to Asher and Chelcie's house for 'family dinner' and my resentment towards everyone around me is getting out of control. Hell, I have no business being out in public with the thoughts I keep thinking. I want to take Maddox by the neck and shake some sense into his thick scull.

I put a brave face on for Chelcie. I smile and keep the act up like my world isn't crashing down around me, but every time my eyes lock with Maddox's, I'm reminded that he is the reason I'm feeling this pain. The fact that he keeps pushing me away is why I've turned into a head case.

Then, as if things couldn't get worse, I have the misfortune of overhearing their conversation and my mood goes from bad to toxic.

Chelcie has just finished telling him how she was dealing with everything after Sarah Jane. I watch her place her arm on his cheek and he doesn't pull away. I should feel bad about eavesdropping, but the fact that he isn't pulling away from her is mind-blowing enough for me.

He's let her in.

He's let in someone I know he feels nothing romantic for, yet he keeps pushing me away.

"One day, Maddox Locke, when you decide to let go of that

pain inside you, you're going to understand what I mean. You have so much love to give in you." Chelcie's words hurt. She's right—I know that because I've seen that love he has the capability of—but it still doesn't make it feel any better knowing that it probably is not meant to be with us.

I can't see his face, but I watch Chelcie's eyes widen in shock. Oh I know what she saw—the truth. She saw his pain clear as day. The pain he keeps away from everyone, choosing to suffer alone and not let anyone close enough to help.

"Yeah, sweetheart. Maybe you're right."

His words are my undoing. He really doesn't want me. Hell, maybe he does believe that he can love someone now—now that he's gotten better about being so untouchable. But… he clearly doesn't feel like I'm worth that risk. I'm standing right here, begging him to let me take on his pain, yet it isn't enough.

With my eyes filling with tears, I watch as he walks right past me. He doesn't even look in my direction. I'm completely invisible.

As the evening progresses, my despair and bitterness grow. I smile with the girls, attempt to put on a brave face for the guys—but Maddox gets nothing. Until I hear Asher announce that he and Chelcie are getting married and he actually has the nerve to look smug. His eyes go from laughing at Chelcie to emotionless when they lock with mine.

I snap… There really isn't a pretty way to explain what I feel in that moment. I'm just…done.

"You're fucking unbelievable," I mumble, careful to keep my voice low enough so that only he hears me.

His brow lifts and he cockily asks, "What was that, Em?"

That son of a bitch. I can feel my skin heat. Not from embarrassment, but from red-hot rage.

I jump from my seat, not even flinching when it falls to the floor with a crowd-stopping boom. I storm over, grabbing his beer for a deep pull while I try and pick my words carefully. If these are the last ones I ever speak to him, I need to make sure they count.

"Look at you. Sitting there silent as always. You're in a room full of people who love each other. People who have fought *their* demons in order to be together. They had the strength to battle anything that stood in their way. The courage to push away from the uncertainty of the unknown. And what does Maddox Locke do? He sits back and gives everyone else around him advice on how to make that happen! He fights for *them*, but he refuses to fight for himself. FOR ME! Well guess what, buddy? I'm sick of it. I love you FOR you. I never gave a damn about your past, those secrets you hide so deep. I've been willing to fight for you. Battle those demons that shake your doors at night. And while I'm at it, I might as well go for broke, right?" I laugh a sound that is nothing sort of the frustration I'm feeling. "I never gave a damn about you having one leg. You think you're slick hiding it, but *I see you!* I didn't love you for whatever limbs you have or don't have. I want you for your heart, and I won't settle for anything less."

I throw him a look that I know he takes seriously because his eyes flash. He doesn't move though. He lets me walk over to Asher and Chelcie. He gives me the time to say goodbye and apologize for ruining the night. He doesn't move when I walk to the door, turning to give him another look. He sits there—and that's it.

Luckily, when we got here, he asked me to hold his keys, so with a wicked grin, I hop in his Charger and take off. I'll stay in a local hotel room for the night—then decide where I go next.

# CHAPTER 16
## Emmy

IT DOESN'T take me long to clear my things from his apartment. I decide to leave Cat, mainly because I have no where to bring her and all the things that she needs, but also so that Maddox will see this as me not running.

I'm not. I'm going to get myself settled away from him and work on learning how to get him out of my heart. I can do it…I think.

My phone rings over and over shortly after I leave Asher and Chelcie's, but I ignore it. I know my window of opportunity is short, and if I stall at all, he will be here and throw his demanding alpha vibes up—refusing to let me leave.

Not wanting to take his Charger and further fuel his anger, I make a call to the only person I can think of who can help me out right now.

Sway.

"Well hello, you dark prince you," his voice chimes through the line, leaving me confused—until I realize that I'm on Maddox's landline.

"Hey," I whisper. "I hate to disappoint you, Sway, but I don't think I'm your dark prince."

"Why do you sound like that, Miss Emmy?"

There aren't many times when we get the Sway he keeps hidden. Deep down, I know he loves us more than we could ever know. Hearing the care and worry in his voice is almost my undoing, but I hold strong.

"Do you think you could pick me up? My car is still… My car isn't here and I need to leave."

"Sure thing, darling girl. Let me get things settled and I'll be right there."

"Thank you, Sway. I owe you one."

"Far as I can see were even, my love."

Confused at his words, I ask, "How could we possible call it even, Sway?"

He's silent for a beat. I can hear him moving around, clearly using this time to pick his words. "Everything happens for a reason, Emmy. I know that now. As much as I hated seeing you gone day in and day out, you brought my Davey to me. So, yes…we're even. If anything, I still owe you," he laughs.

I heard about Davey, or David, through the gang. He is my replacement at Corps Security. Apparently, according to Melissa, not too long after he started, he and Sway began a relationship that has only grown since. I'm glad that he's happy—he deserves to be happy.

"I'll be in the lobby waiting, okay?" I question, ready to get off the phone and on my way.

"Toodles! Sway is on the way to save the day," he giggles into the phone before disconnecting.

With a heavy heart, I grab a piece of paper and write Maddox a note.

True to his word, Sway didn't waste any time getting to me. He loaded up my few belongings into his car and we were on our way. He must have come straight from home because he's dressed in simple—even if they are hot pink—sweats and a tee. His wig is absent, giving me one of those rare glimpses at him without his public persona.

"Sway…uh, do you really, like, sweat glitter or something?" I ask when I notice that his floorboards are sprinkled with golden glitter.

I've always thought it was hilarious how obsessed this man is with gold glitter. First, he painted the sidewalk in the complex that his salon and Corps Security are housed completely in it. Then the guys would randomly run into him and his glitter-throwing ways, coming into the office and dusting it off all over the floors. I can't even remember how many times I had to clean that junk up. Regardless of why, it always seems to make everyone smile.

"I probably should by now," he laughs.

Not wanting to be alone with my thoughts, I tell him which hotel to take me to and ask, "So what started all of this craziness?" I laugh.

He's quiet for a moment, so unlike Sway, so I turn my attention back out the window.

"It all started when I was maybe fifteen, sixteen—hell, I don't know. Back then, I was still begging for my parents to stop calling me Dilbert," he laughs. "My parents are both preachers," he says, shocking me. My eyes widen and I jerk my head in his direction. "Oh, that got your attention, didn't it, sweetness? Yeah, I was a black man born in the Deep South, gay as it gets, with two preachers for parents. It probably couldn't have gotten worse for me. They ignored me the best they could but refused to let...well, Sway out. I had to be Dilbert when anyone was around." He pauses and I settle into the silence around me.

"The only time I was really happy was at Sunday school, at school, or drama class. The art supplies—oh, girlfriend. You should have seen how much I could make a simple piece of construction paper shine like a queen! I guess, in a way, between art projects and costumes for drama, the glitter became my lifeline to keeping my happiness about me. We all have that thing, you know? That one thing that is calming for us. The one thing that, even when your world feels hollow, can make you feel whole. So, as silly as it is, mine is gold glitter. It's my happy."

I wipe a wayward tear from my cheek and smile softly at him. "You're pretty awesome. You know that?"

He laughs and shakes his head.

"I mean it! Do you know how many times the guys would be in a terrible mood, go out and meet with a client, only to come back and be on the receiving end of your glitter throwing? Every single time, they would come back into the office and seem lighter. It was almost like a mood cleaner. You toss some of that stuff in the air and it's like the people around you are helpless to not feel a little of your happy."

He pulls into the hotel and parks, turning in his seat to look at me. One thick and manicured hand comes up and smooths my hair down. I smile at him and enjoy the lightness of the moment.

Until he speaks.

"And pray tell, my sweet little honey pot, what is your happy?" His hand leaves my head and reaches out to pull one of my cold ones into his hold, enveloping it between his own.

"What?" I ask faintly.

"You heard me. What is it that calms you? Makes your hollow whole again?" His voice is soft, his eyes searching without judgment—even though he knows the answer.

"I don't have one anymore, Sway." That's as honest as I can be. I never had Maddox, as much as I had hoped during our time at the cabin. He's the uncatchable.

"Oh, you sweet child. You have a happy, and as soon as you both let go of the bullshit, you'll have that happy together."

"You talk in riddles, you crazy man," I laugh mirthlessly.

"I talk the truth. I've seen a lot of pain in my life, Emmy-Rose. I know another hurting soul when I see it, and that man is hurting. You don't just forget that instantly. You've fought for him, and while I admire your strength, it's time for you to let *him* fight to believe in *you* and that love…that happy."

"Easier said than done."

He smiles, his bright, white teeth almost glowing in the dim interior of his car. "Mark my words, he knows what he can have, and one day soon, you're going to wonder what it's like to breathe without that tall glass of hotness on your toes. I suspect you won't wait much longer either." He leans forward and kisses my forehead.

"I love you. You know that?"

"Of course I do, darlin'. Everyone loves Sway," he says with a laugh.

I climb out of the car and meet him around the back, grabbing my stuff from the trunk and placing it on the luggage cart. His arms are around me before I can even say thank you and goodbye.

"Chin up, buttercup," he whispers in my ear, and I feel a rush of calming peace settle over me.

A few hours, one dead cell phone, and room service later, I'm ready to call it a night. I have plans to spend tomorrow figuring out where the hell I go now. Do I stick around, continue this tiring battle of the wills with Maddox? Or do I work on finding a new path—a path without Maddox and the family I love here?

I know I'm stupid to continue to find something worth fighting for in Maddox. He's made it clear that he doesn't want me—or better yet, that he does but he *can't*, whatever that means. I might never get through to him, but I really feel like if I don't try at least one more time—with everything I have in me—I'll regret it for the rest of my life.

He needs someone to believe in him, and I'm guessing he's never had that. He needs someone who never gives up on him, since I'm guessing that's all he's been used to the vast majority of his life.

He needs his 'happy,' as Sway calls it.

And I just hope it's me.

I fall asleep as soon as my head hits the pillow with the determination that I can do this. I just have to toughen up a little, chin up, and YOLO.

*"That's it, buttercup."*

# CHAPTER 17
## *Maddox*

WHAT A fucking mess. I should have known that, the second I got my head out of my ass and allowed myself to believe a little in what I could have, she'd snap. She gives me everything I have been working to get since I started foolishly pushing her away.

The second she finished reaming my ass, that flickering flame of hope burst into an inferno.

She's right; I hid behind playing some twisted matchmaker. Fixing my friends around me, all the while falling deeper into myself. I used their issues to distract them from me. I used each and every one of them to keep them out.

"Uh, where is your car, brother?" Greg snickers from behind me.

"Looks like he was too busy being a giant ass and it got swiped right from under him," Asher laughs.

"Hilarious," I say, not turning from where I'm looking at the space where my Charger should be parked. My lips twitch at the thought of my sweet little Emmy stealing my car.

"That's what you get for pissing her off," Axel laughs.

I shrug my shoulder, not willing to get into this with them. It really shouldn't matter; all but Asher have seen me at my worst, so this is a walk in the park for them.

"Just out of curiosity, is this when we all take the advice you've been giving us for *years* now and give it back? Because hey, I'm not a chick, so I'm not really sure how these little special moments are supposed to go, but I'm willing to wing it."

They all laugh when Beck chimes in. I turn and take in the four men standing in front of me, meeting each of their eyes to figure out what I'm supposed to say.

"Maddox Locke?" a little voice calls from behind the guys.

"Yeah, C-Man?" I should have known that Cohen, Greg and Melissa's son, would find us out here. He's been one of the guys ever since he went through some crazy shit a few years ago.

"I thought you were gonna bring Aunt Emmy home forever and ever."

"Leave it to the kid to say what we're all thinking."

I don't know who said it; I'm too busy looking at Cohen, his expressive, brown eyes locked with mine.

"You're a big, brave superhero, Maddox Locke. I know it because you helped me bring my mommy back. You told me I needed to be brave and strong and show her my love. That's all you have to do. When Mommy is mad at Daddy, he just tickles her until they start making funny noises." He puts his small, balled-up fist on his hips and gives Greg as hard a look as he can when he starts choking on his laughter. "I bet if you smiled real big like that she would like that. You don't smile a lot, Maddox Locke."

I clear my throat and look up at the guys for some help. They all seem to be just as shocked with how much the little dude takes in from all of us.

"Yeah, C-Man, I think you're right. I might even try that smiling stuff you're talking about."

"Woohoo!" he yells, spinning on his small feet and slapping my body with his cape that is always tied around his neck. "Mommy! Aunt Dee! He said I was right and he's gonna *smile*!" he screams, running back in the house.

I lock eyes with the guys, each of us struggling to hold it in, before we all burst out laughing. It feels so foreign to me that I have to wonder, *is this what happiness feels like?*

"You want me to give you a lift? Chelcie can handle things before I get back," Asher asks when the others go back inside.

"Yeah, brother. I'd like that."

He smiles, gives me a nod, and runs inside to get the keys to his Jeep.

The ride back to the apartment is pretty quiet. I know it's not going to last long; Asher isn't exactly a silent thinker. Sometimes, I swear the wheels can be heard clanking around in his head before he even gets his words out. I guess part of the way he and Coop grew up taught him to pick his words carefully, and I can respect that, so I give him the time he needs.

Well, at least I try to give him the time he needs—it isn't like I live hours away.

"Just spit it out, Asher. I know you have something to say, so you might as well get it out before we hit the apartment complex, because the second you roll up there, I'm out."

"Right," he starts. "So…that picture I found?"

"That's all you want to ask me? About a picture you found weeks ago in a forgotten box deep in my closet?" I clarify.

"Well, I was just wondering if your nightmare—you know you called that picture that—had gotten better."

"I'm working on it," I tell him honestly.

"And do you remember when you told me to wake up and realize there's more to live for? I know you've seen some shit, Mad. Otherwise, you wouldn't have been able to hit so close to home with your words months ago. You once told me to stop beating myself up over things I had no control over, and the Maddox Locke I know is no goddamn hypocrite, so I have to ask—are you done with your shit?"

I keep looking at his profile for a second, noticing for the first time just how nervous he was to throw all that out there. Then, for the second time tonight, I throw my head back and laugh.

"Yeah, Asher. You know what they say: YOLO."

It's pretty ridiculous that it takes a five-year-old kid to make me wake the hell up and take a chance. Jesus, I can't believe I just fucking said 'YOLO.'

The Jeep swerves slightly when his head jerks in my direction. "Did you just YOLO me?"

Still laughing, I reply, "Yeah, asshole. Someone wise once told me that was the best way to live your life."

He smiles sadly for a second, knowing damn well there was only one of our group who would ever willingly say YOLO.

The rest of the drive, we make small talk, but my nerves are too jumpy for me to really engage in any sort of conversation with him. I know I have a long road to go. I'm not instantly going to just be able to forget my past, but from this moment forward, I have to be willing to take a chance. I have to take a chance at what Emmy has been offering me and pray that I'm making the right decision.

Because I don't think I'll be able to live with myself if my demons make my angel fall.

"There's the Charger," he says, breaking the silence we adopted about five minutes ago.

"Yup."

"Do you need anything else?"

"Nope, I'm good—but I'll let you know if that changes," I say, stepping down from the Jeep. I turn back before I shut the door and let my lips tip up. "Thanks for…everything."

His eyes flash at the shock of my words. "Yeah, any time. If you need me, just call."

I nod my head, shut his door, and stride to the elevators. The garage is silent for the night, the majority of the tenants in the apartment complex home from wherever they've been—settled in for a night of relaxing. Not me though. Nope. Tonight, I'm going to claim my woman for good.

It's time to let my angel in and hope that she can really help me battle all of this shit I carry around with me like dead weight.

# CHAPTER 18
## *Maddox*

THE FIRST thing I notice when I step into my apartment is the silence. Usually, I can always hear her tinkering around, even when she isn't doing anything physically. Her soft singing, the pages of her book turning, or even the humming noises she makes when she's asleep.

Cat greets me at the door with a deep meow, as usual. We've developed some weird friendship. Emmy used to laugh and say that Cat could recognize someone who needed a friend. Oh how right she was. I scratch Cat behind the ears and set off to look for her owner.

"Em?"

Nothing. A flash of apprehension over the situation starts to take over, but I push it aside and keep looking for her. The apartment isn't huge, but it's large enough that she might not have heard me.

A few minutes later, I realize that she really isn't here. After walking into my bedroom, I sit on my bed and think about where the hell she could have gone. She doesn't have her car because we still haven't gotten it back from the cabin. I had Greg and Asher swing down and bring it back, knowing that, if I got anywhere near that place, I wouldn't be leaving until there was blood on the ground. Devon said that we could leave it there as long as we needed, and since he wouldn't be back for a few weeks, I haven't been in any kind of rush. I liked having her dependent on me to get places.

With a deep sigh, I lean back and let my head hit the pillow—only to shoot back up when my head hits something besides the pillow.

I reach out with a shaking hand and pick up the note with my name written in Emmy's flowing handwriting. I don't want to open it, dreading what could be inside, but if I have any hopes of finding her tonight, this would be where to start.

*Dear Maddox,*

*I used to think that my love for you would be strong enough for both of us. Some sort of weird platform that could hold anything you threw at me—and never break. I know now that I was sadly mistaken.*

*For as long as I've known you, I've felt a pull towards you like I've never known before. It's no secret now that I haven't had the best of beginnings in my life. Even with all of that in my past, I still had faith in love. Maybe I just had rose-colored glasses on. I'm not sure. But I wanted to believe that there was some sort of reward to be had for all the bullshit I had to deal with to get here.*

*I'm only human, Maddox. I'm not sure how many times it will take of you pushing me away before you start kicking me while I'm down—I bleed just like the rest of us when I fall...only when I fall at your hands, it hurts just a little more. I fear that I'm no lon-*

*ger strong enough to stand against your continuous rejection—to stand on the sidelines and watch you willing to fight for everyone one else around us to get their slice of happiness.*

*One thing I know for sure now is that, as much as I wish it were different, I can't keep begging you to believe in us. I'm sure that my heart will undoubtedly always belong to you—my dark prince. But until you can see just how worthy your love is, I'm afraid I just don't have a part in your life.*

*I want you to know that I'm not running. Not from you and not from my life here. But I can't be around you. When you're in the room, I instantly want to run into your arms and beg you to let me all the way in. To let me help you carry some of the baggage, slay the demons—to let me help you heal. So, for right now, I'm going to get a hotel room and fix my head...and my heart. I know Cat is in good hands until I can get settled. I'm pretty sure she likes you more than me anyway.*

*I love you.*

*I wish you knew how much.*

*-Em*

Her words crash over me, leaving me hollow and alone. I rub my chest, feeling some weird burn taking over my lungs. She can't just give up. Not my Emmy.

Although, I'm not sure why I even doubt that she could. This is, after all, everything I've been working towards for years. I pushed her away and refused the love she so desperately wanted to hand me.

I pace my room, wondering when the hell I'm supposed to

stop. I refuse to sit here on my ass when she needs me. She needs me to prove to her that I'm going to let her in. I know that, if I don't make this next move flawlessly, she will never believe that I'm willing to give it a go.

"Fuck!" I bellow, pulling my arm back and slamming it into the wall. The drywall gives way and I watch my fist sink right through. If anything, it just feeds my mood, makes me want to start destroying everything until I find her.

I'll fucking turn this town on its ass to find her.

An hour later, I've basically torn my place apart looking for some kind of clue and I'm not any closer. Her stuff is gone. Everything except the things Cat needs and the lingering sweetness of her smell is gone. I'm coming unglued, and if I don't get some kind of sign soon, I'm going to snap.

I throw my body down on the couch and take in the room. Everything is where it was when we left earlier. The remote is on the table. The magazine she had been flipping through before we left is sitting in the chair I've started thinking of as hers. The candles she bought to make my place smell like a damn apple pie sit unlit on the counter next to the phone…

The phone that isn't on the cradle, where I know I put it earlier. I jump up from the couch and walk into the kitchen, spying the cordless lying on the counter. With a pleading prayer that maybe this is the clue I need to figure out where she went, I grab it and press redial.

I know that number.

Sway.

Not wasting a second, I quickly press the on button and wait for him to pick up. God, I hate this feeling of being out of control of everything around me.

"Hello?" David's voice comes through the line and I want to scream.

"Where is he?"

"Hello to you too, Maddox," he laughs, getting a growl out of me in return.

"Yeah, hello, David… Where is Sway?"

"He got back a second ago, and I'm guessing, since you're calling now, that you're wondering where Emmy is?"

"You would be correct," I grind through my clenched jaw.

"Hold on. Let me go get him."

I hear him moving around and then speaking softly. I wait, trying my hardest not to snap the phone in half with the force of my grip.

"Well hello there, you sexy man. If only I would have known how popular I would become tonight. You're lucky we decided to leave in the morning to go to Davey's parent's house. Did you hear? I'm meeting the parents." He sighs deeply, and I growl again, hoping he takes a hint and gets to the point.

"Where is she?"

"Right to the point, I see. Well, my hunk of silence, she's safe."

He just stops talking, and I'm seconds away from blowing up on him. I know he doesn't deserve my wrath, so I try to push it down.

And fail.

"Sway! Where in the hell is my woman? I need to fucking find her two hours ago!"

"AH! Now that's just what I needed to hear, sweet cheeks.

You know, I've been waiting for the moment when you would let the smoke clear out of your delectable ass. You've been so foolish. So Sway is going to help you out now, and please, Maddox, do not make me regret this. That girl deserves her slice of happiness, and you're lucky that I feel like that is you. You can find her at the Marriott over on Brookfield. I watched her walk through the doors and check in with my own eyes—so, my love, that is where you're going to go get your woman. You can thank Sway later. Toodles!" He giggles softly as he hangs up.

Two seconds later, I'm out the door and making my way to my Charger.

# CHAPTER 19
## Emmy

THE POUNDING at the door wakes me after what feels like just two seconds of sleeping. My whole body feels like it weighs a hundred extra pounds. I should have known that Sway wouldn't keep his mouth shut. I was so focused on getting the hell out before Maddox came home that I didn't give a second thought to who helped me.

I stand at the door, my forehead planted against the wood, and breathe deeply. I have to remember that, whatever he says to me in anger, he doesn't mean. He never means it. I can tell when he's looking right at me that his eyes are begging for me not to believe what comes out of his mouth. I have to stay strong and let him know that he's off the hook. He won't have to deal with my stupid love anymore.

"Open the door, Emersyn."

His voice hits me with a force so powerful that, even through the thick door, it makes me shiver. *Stay strong, Emmy. You can do this. Just let him know that you're done.*

Wrapping my fingers around the door handle, feeling the cold steel against my skin, I try to let it center me. One last little push to stand strong and put a cold layer of ice over my heart.

I swing the door open right when he's about to knock again and his fist stops just inches from my face. I gasp.

"Shit," he growls.

We stand there just looking into each other's eyes. I have no idea what's going through his head right now. Why he's even here. I said everything I needed to in that letter—unless he didn't get it. Shit. I don't think I'm going to be able to get that all out to his face. Writing it all down about killed me.

He's still wearing the clothes from earlier—a dark-green Henley and jeans that are worn in all the right places. The sleeves are rolled up to his elbows, showing off the weaving lines of his tattoos. Reds and blacks dance together over almost every inch of his forearms. I know the design travels up both arms and ends by wrapping slightly around the back right on the base of his neck. Depending on the shirt, sometimes I can see a few of the lines licking up his tan skin. I've studied his forearms for so long that I imagine each and every sweep the tattoo gun must have taken. I know he has more along his ribs, but I've never had the pleasure to study them. I just know that it's more blacks and reds.

When he clears his throat, I move my gaze from his thick, muscled forearms to meet his eyes. His deep-brown, very worried eyes. He isn't masking his feelings from me right now, and as shocked as I am, I'm more confused than ever.

"What are you doing here?"

I haven't let go of the door handle, using it to help hold my body from falling to the floor. He stands before me, still in the hallway, and at my question, he looks to his left and then right before meeting my gaze again. This time, the worry is replaced with… determination?

In a move so quick that I gasp, he's pushing his way into the room and helping the door shut with a kick. I back up as he stalks towards me, my eyes wide and my breathing erratic.

"Maddox?" I implore.

"This is you not running?" he questions, solidifying that he did, in fact, read the letter I'd left him. "You think I haven't felt that pull? Jesus, Emmy, it's so strong that I feel like I'm being sucked into a vortex. I've pushed and pushed, not to reject you—even though I now see my mistake—but to protect you. That love that you've been offering, I want nothing more than to take it and run. I have so many demons, Emmy. So many that they are woven into my very being, and I'm goddamn terrified that, if I take what you're offering, even the platform, that promise of love, that you've been building won't be strong enough, and when I tumble down, I'll take you with me—straight into the pits of hell."

He forces out a laugh and bends slightly at his waist, his hands going to his neck and his fingers clenching in frustration.

"Your words play in my head night after night, and fuck me if I didn't recognize it before now, but you've been fighting those damn demons back even without knowing it." He steps closer, and I have no energy to move back. I stand still, shock rooting me in place, and try to desperately process his words. "Someone told me earlier tonight that I needed to be brave and strong and show you my love. Laid out there in black and white by a damn kid," he laughs. "He pulled my head out of my ass in two seconds, Em."

"Mad—" I start.

"No, Em, let me finish. It's not going to be easy for me, this whole getting words out when I've spend so long training myself to keep them in. For you, though… For you, I'm going to try, yeah?"

I nod and wait for him to continue. Both of us stand there, so close yet so far.

"The day I met you, my body was screaming to run. I hadn't felt like that…ever. You brought out every single emotion that I had been fighting to keep locked away. I've feared every second since that those holds would never be strong enough against you. Jesus, Em, you have to understand this is new to me."

"I know that, Mad," I whisper.

"I pushed you. I hurt you—God, I hurt you—because I could never live with myself if the demons, the darkness, the *evil* inside me harmed you."

"So you just decided to do it yourself? Save your stupid demons of darkness the trouble and just handle it?" I snip at him.

He at least has the decency to flinch. "Something like that, Em. It's all I know. It's the only way I could think to protect you and that was a vast mistake on my end. I want to let you in, Em. Fuck—I'm willing to goddamn beg if that's what it takes for you to just believe that I'm here and craving just a sliver of your love. I honestly don't know how to make it any clearer."

"Just like that, Maddox? You want me to believe that, just like that, with one snap of my fingers, you're going to be able to miraculously let me the hell in? Because I'm sorry, but I'm not buying it. I can only take so much before I've just had enough. I'm not even sure if I have the fight left in me for the both of us."

His eyes close at my words and his head drops slightly. "No, Em, I don't expect you to just believe me like that. But let's get one thing straight—it doesn't matter if you have any fight left in you because I'm going to fight hard enough for both of us now, angel. It's time for you to hand over all of that strength and maybe give me a few pointers, but it's time…time to let *me* fight for *us.*"

I gasp, tears forming and rolling over my eyes without my permission. He doesn't even give them a chance to fall before he takes his hands and frames my face, kissing each one as quickly as he can.

"Please don't give up on me," he whimpers.

That sound coming out of him is my undoing. A deep sob bubbles past my throat and I wrap my arms around him and hold him tight.

Our grips on each other don't weaken. My tears soak his shirt and his breathing never slows, his heart beating rapidly against my cheek. I want so desperately to believe him, to take this lifeline that he's thrown my way, but I'm scared.

The doubts and fears of what happens when he stops believing in us are almost too much. I need to think. I need to get my head together without him around, and even though I want to beg him to stay and take the comfort his arms are offering, I have to take this time—even if it is just tonight—and figure out once and for all if this is a road I can continue down.

Pulling back, I meet his eyes and tell him the only thing I can right now. "I need time, Maddox. I'm not asking for a lot, but just give me tonight…please."

"I'm not fucking leaving, Emersyn." His tone leaves no room for argument, but I know that, if he really means what he just said, he's going to have to learn to give a little and not take it all.

"You really don't have a choice right now, do you?"

His eyes darken, but I press on.

"Just a few hours ago, I cried myself to sleep with the knowledge that I had to give you up. I had talked myself into learning how to move on from everything I've fought for. That isn't something I can just turn off with a few words. Even if they're words I've craved. I meant what I said earlier in my letter—I bleed just like the rest of us. And right now, you need to go home and let me patch up those wounds and *THINK.*"

"It's going against everything my body is demanding I do to make you believe me to just leave," he pleads.

"Unfortunately for you, Maddox, right now, you don't have a say. I need this time."

He doesn't speak, his eyes begging me to give in so fiercely that I have to move out of his hold and take a step back. His face drops with my movement and the truth sinks in. I'm not just giving in, and as much as it's killing me not to, I need to make sure. If he is willing to give me this, then maybe he's willing to really fight.

"I'll give you tonight, angel, but I'll be back. When the sun comes up, I'm going to be right back at your door, and I hope to God you will see then that I'm serious. I'm trying—I just need you to get some of that believe in us back and hold my hand as I go… because I'm going in blind, baby."

I close my eyes and nod. He gives me one last pleading glance before moving towards me. He brushes his finger over my lips, trailing it down my neck before placing his hand over my heart.

"I want this back, and I'm going to do everything I can to have it." He gives me one soft kiss before walking towards the door.

I get one more sad smile before he's gone.

Then I crumble to the floor and cry. Everything I've wanted is right there—but will I be able to take a chance knowing that I might crash and break down even harder if he changes his mind?

# CHAPTER 20
## Emmy

I SHOULD HAVE known that I would never be able to sleep with the thoughts that are spinning around in my head. Ultimately, I know which side will win. I still need to make sure that I'm ready to put myself out there, to take a blind chance, but then again if I don't, then I will be proving to him that he was right all along. I'll prove to him that the gift of his love means nothing to me.

And when it's put that way, there is no way I can do that. I might regret it, giving him this last chance, but at least if I'm left without him in the end of it, I'll know that I gave it my all.

He left a few hours ago, and after I was able to pull myself off the floor, I took a long and hot shower, using the time to get all my fears and hopes in order. If this works out, then everything I've known we could be together will be ours, and just the thought has me smiling.

Throwing back the covers, I take a look at the clock. Four in the morning. He'll be here soon and I'm almost nervous to tell him that I'm ready. That, together, we will get through his darkness—and those damn demons he thinks are so prevalent that he has to keep others away.

A knock at the door has my head whipping around; of course he wouldn't be able to stay away. I'm actually shocked he lasted the last six hours.

Straightening my tank top and making sure that my sleep shorts aren't hanging off my ass, I walk to the door, taking a deep breath to calm my nerves.

Then I swing the door open with a smile—a smile that quickly dies when I see who is standing on the other side.

"Princess," Shawn slurs. "Aren't you a hard little bitch to track down." His evil makes my skin crawl.

I can feel the bile in my stomach threatening to make its way up and I sway on my feet.

How did he find me? We were so careful from the beginning. When I first got away, Coop and Axel hid not only the trail, but every trace of me. I worked under the table. I had a credit and debit card under the company name. Even my apartment was in Coop's name.

Holy shit! That's when my own stupidity literally slaps me in the face. When I went back, I opened a bank account so I could get the hotel room, making it no secret where I was since they knew I was back.

And I didn't touch it again…until last night.

Oh, God, why now? Why, when everything was starting to look up, does he have to show up?! Just when I started to believe that I could have it all.

"Have nothing to say to me? Well, I have to plenty to say to you, bitch."

His heavy palm hits me between my breast first, knocking the wind from my lungs and my legs right out from under me. As I crash to the floor, his laugh wraps around me like a noose.

"Little Syn, living up to her name by playing house with that motherfucker who took you from me when I wasn't looking. Did you fucking think I would sit back and let you go? I don't fucking think so," he fumes, his spit flying from the force of his words and falling on my face. "You belong to me, bitch."

I move to stand—to just get away from the disadvantage I have from being on the floor as he towers over me—but I'm stopped short when his heavy, booted foot presses against my chest. I can feel my ribs protesting against the pressure, crying out for some relief.

"I'm going to teach you a lesson first, Syn."

When his foot comes off my chest, I crab-crawl backwards until my head hits hard against the desk in the corner. I go to scream, but guessing my intent, he jumps and his body crashing into mine renders me silent. My body is drowning under the panic he elicits.

His hand grips my neck, digging in and curling his fingers—choking me in a brutal hold. I gasp, my eyes watering at the pain. My fingers tear at his skin, and when that doesn't work, I bring my hand weakly up to his face and claw him. My fingers score his skin, leaving four deep marks across his face from temple to chin.

"You fucking bitch!" he roars and brings his fist down, hitting me right in the cheek.

My head snaps to the side, but I fight the blackness that is hedging in. I won't fucking give in. Not this time—not when I have every reason to *fight* him.

He's always wanted this—this fight—and he's going to get it.

I give him everything I have. His fist hits me every time I move my arms from my face to deliver one of my own. Then I feel my left arm split in one powerful punch, making it harder to defend myself. When he leaves his guard down, I slam my knee into his crotch, knocking him to his side. As quickly as I can, I start to crawl away, opening my mouth to call out for help only to have a hoarse rasp come out. My efforts are weak since I'm dragging my body with one arm. Each time I put pressure on my left side, my arm gives out.

His laughter starts to taunt me and the fear almost consumes me. Every inch of my body hurts, but I'm not giving up. He won't have me this time. Not when the future is right within my grasp.

"Get the fuck back here," he snarls when I unsteadily climb to my feet.

The second I have my footing, he brings his leg out and sweeps me right back on my ass. I fall with bone-jarring force, the wind once again knocked from my body. The tears and snot running down my face are making it hard for me to even see, let alone breathe, so every breath I've been conserving rapidly throws me off.

He climbs on top of me, straddling my waist, pulling my arms over my head, and clamping them tight within one of his own—the other going to my mouth to make sure I don't cry out. Even if I wanted to, I couldn't. My throat is raw from when he choked me earlier. The pain from my broken arm produces a wave of nausea to roll through me, causing me to vomit all over myself.

He doesn't even notice, his all-consuming rage to the point where I know he's not going to stop until he's gotten everything he can from me. "I've had to sit back and wait for this moment. Wait for you to finally fuck up and lead me right to you. I knew it would happen—you never were very fucking bright. I'll give you credit.

You got away once, and had you not come crawling back to me, I might not have found you. I don't fucking like to wait, Syn, and it's about time you learned who is your goddamn boss! You think you're fucking smart, running off again? I won't let you get away this time. Not when the club needs your cunt to make the money keep coming in."

When his hand comes back to my throat, I see it in his eyes—he doesn't care if I live past this moment as long as he gets whatever sick shit he wants.

"Just like a sitting duck," he spits in my face. "The second your credit card was used, it was like a big fucking flag just taking me right to your door. Where's your big, bad savior now? Doesn't look like he's going to help you this time, you senseless fucking bitch!"

The pressure in my chest demanding oxygen is becoming too much. My eyes are starting to close despite my willing them to keep focused. And worse, my limbs have stopped listening to my command to fight, just dropping lifelessly to my side.

"This is going to be so much fun, you stupid bitch." He brings his hand back, and with one hard punch to my temple, I'm out cold.

I'm not sure how long I'm out. When I come to, I fight with myself to get past the fog. My head is pounding and my body is sore. Without opening my eyes, I take stock of my body. I hurt, but nothing that makes me too concerned. The fact that I can feel that my clothing has been torn from my body, however, is enough for me to become instantly terrified. Between all my pains and aches, it's hard to tell if he took me, but I'm almost positive that he hasn't raped me…yet.

I hear a phone ring, a tone I know is not mine, and I breathe a sigh a relief when Shawn stops what he is doing, climbs off me, and answers the phone.

"What?" he barks farther away from where I'm laying.

After a brief silence, I hear him and my heart stops.

"Yeah, I fucking got her, Ram, and don't you fucking worry. When I'm done with her, she won't pull this shit again."

Oh. My. God.

My own father orchestrated this. I shouldn't be surprised. He's never exactly acted like he gave a damn, but knowing that he sent this monster after me is devastating. I know it sounds stupid, to still hope that the father who willingly objectifies his own daughter might care just a little—but like the dreamer I am, I couldn't help but pray that, one day, he would. I know now how foolish that was.

"Yeah, you're damn right she begged. I'll set her straight. Don't you fucking worry. Don't even sweat it, Ram. Come tomorrow morning—or night—I'll be headed back there and then you can let the other boys take their turn with her. Seems about right after all the trouble her little boy toy caused."

When I hear his voice get farther away, I know this is my moment. Peeking my eyes open and seeing his shadow falling from the open doorway of the bathroom gives me the time I need. I move as quickly as my body will allow and get to the hotel phone. After snatching it off the cradle, I press '0' and wait. When I hear the operator answer, I whisper my room number, begging for them to send help quickly. Then I shove the phone beside the bed and the nightstand and make my way to where I left my cell charging on the desk, fumbling for a second as I listen to Shawn laugh at whatever my father is saying.

Laughing about destroying his own flesh and blood.

I manage to get my phone turned on and the phone app open to dial Maddox before I hear Shawn coming behind me. I quickly toss the phone to the side, praying that I pressed the button to connect the call before I had to abandon it.

"Little bitch is awake now, Ram. It's time for me to have some fucking fun before I bring her home." He laughs again.

I curl into a ball when he gives me a hard kick, landing his boot right into my shin. I cry out in pain, my voice still sounding foreign to my ears. He gives me another kick, clearly enjoying the fact that he's hurt me. The pain is overwhelming this time and I get sick again. I'm not even sure what wetness on my body is from vomit, blood, or my tears.

"You going to fight me again, slut? This cunt is mine, and I'm done playing games. It's time for you to remember exactly who you belong to. You're never going to be more than Syn—and even if that bastard got some grand idea to come after you again, he wouldn't want you when I'm finished anyway."

He towers over me, grabbing me by my hair and hauling me from the floor. Then he slaps me across the face before shoving me onto the bed. I fight again, ignoring the pain in my arm and leg, kicking and slapping, but in the end, he's just too strong for me. I'm not sure how long I was able to fight him. It feels like an eternity, and with his hand back on my throat, I pass out, praying that help isn't too far away.

# CHAPTER 21
## *Maddox*

COMING BACK to the apartment without Emmy wasn't how I'd seen the night ending. As foolish as it was to believe that we could just fall back into whatever we had before, but I hadn't anticipated her telling me to leave. It took one hell of a battle with my mind to get my feet to leave that room. To get my legs to carry me out of the hotel and into my car. It took even longer to convince my mind to leave her there.

I took care of feeding Cat and cleaning out her litter box when I got in. Then I set off to pick up the rest of the apartment since I had torn it up while looking for a clue as to where she was.

And then I was left sitting on the couch, staring at the clock as it ticked each painfully slow second by. Mocking me with the knowledge that I couldn't make time go by more quickly.

I must have fallen asleep because the sound of my phone ringing jolts me with a start. Noticing that the time is just a few hours before dawn, I make my way down the hall to grab my screaming phone.

When I see her name across the screen, my heart skips a beat. She could be telling me not to bother or calling to tell me to come back. Either way, I'm nervous—a feeling I have no idea what to do with.

"Em," I greet, my lips tipping up in a smile.

I don't hear anything for a few beats…until a voice that I know damn well doesn't belong on this call comes through the line.

My heart stops. Right now, the blood just stops moving through my body and a rage I've never known consumes me.

While I race to the elevator, knowing that my leg will never hold up if I storm down twenty-seven flights of stairs, I try to calm my mind and go into fight mode. As hard as it's going to be, I need to think about this as objectively as I can in order to get her out of there. Treat her like a hostage who has the clock against her—which is exactly what I'm dealing with.

It's almost impossible to put my feelings for Emmy aside and focus on how to save her, but it's my only chance. I keep the phone trained to my ear, listening to the muffed hell she is living. I use the sounds to fuel my rage and determination. If I stop for just a second and let the helplessness of the situation sink in, I know I'll be no good to her. I need that rage, the years of hate and injustice, to be my weapon.

This is my chance to let every one of the demons—the monsters in my soul—free and let the wrath consume my body.

I reach the garage level in minutes. Minutes that, in reality, felt like hours, but less than a second after the doors open, I'm sprinting as fast as I can towards my Charger. My phone is still glued to my ear as I listen to the muffled fight.

Then I'm rushing through the streets as fast as I can push my car, my eyes focused like tunnel vision on one thing.

Obliterating the motherfucker who dared to put his hands on my sweet angel.

It takes me five minutes and twenty-six seconds to get to the hotel. I jump out of the car before I even have a chance to throw it in park, not even giving a fuck that it's rolling towards the brick pillar holding up the covered carport. I jump and fucking run.

"Give me the keycard for room four seventeen," I demand, my eyes wild as I take in the terrified night clerk. She doesn't move. "Fucking hell! NOW!"

"I ca-can't give you access, sir," she stutters.

"There's a sadistic, abusive, FUCKING RAPIST up there right now with my woman, so let me tell you again—give me the goddamn keycard!" My voice booms through the lobby.

Her eyes go wide as she fumbles with the stack of cards next to her computer. "We got a call down not even ten minutes ago. I thought it was a joke, so I hung up."

I'm sorry—what? I'm having a hard time following her, keeping my attention to the noises coming through my cell, and seeing through my adrenaline-filled, raging mind.

"Give me the card and you better fucking pray I'm not too late," I threaten.

She fucking hung up. She had enough time to make two calls and only one came.

"NOW!" I bellow when it takes her a second longer.

With a shaking hand, she hands the card over. I keep my eyes trained on her and show her just how dangerous I am.

"Stairs?" I bark. She points and I take off. "And fucking call the police!"

Knowing that she is just four flights of stairs away and I'm just seconds away from her gives me the added push that I need to stretch the limits of my body. I don't have the right prosthetic for running on —every heavy step I take pinches the skin around my stump, but all that pain does is help power my determination.

It drives me, my demons, and the fear I have for her to the brink of dominance over my body. I'm in control here, and that motherfucker better watch out.

I move swiftly down the short hallway until I'm standing outside her door. Not knowing if he is armed has me at a disadvantage, but I'm trained for this—trained to kill—and there isn't anything that can stop me now. I drop my phone in the hallway and ready myself for whatever I might find inside her room.

Leaning my ear against the door as I slowly and silently push the card into the slot gives me a clue that he's going to be at least away from the door. The deep vibrations of his voice are muffled enough that I guess he's a good ten feet from the doorway.

Thank fuck the lock is almost silent when I slowly pull the handle down and push the door open. Entering the small hallway, I see one of her legs hanging off the bed at an odd angle. Her arm is lying next to her body, unmoving. When I see the amount of blood and bile around the floor in front of the bed, I flip the switch and let the monsters take control.

When I set them free, I throw years of pain, hurt, and suffering into my actions. I channel every second I've every felt unworthy of anything to save my angel.

Taking him by surprise is a huge advantage. He's balancing on his hand, with the other stroking his pathetic dick as he sucks on my angel's exposed and bruised breast. Her panties are still on—even if they're hanging by a ripped thread—and I feel instant relief that I might have gotten here quickly enough to make sure this doesn't get any worse.

"You. Motherfucker," I grind out, my saliva frothing at the corners of my lips when I take a good look at Emmy. "I'm going to fucking kill you!"

He has the nerve to laugh, standing from the bed with his dick still bobbing in front of him. He charges, but his movements aren't coordinated and he stumbles the second his pants get around his knees. That gives me the opening I need.

Grabbing his head between my palms, I slam his head down on my knee. He cries out, falling to the floor before jumping back up. He gets a swift uppercut to the temple, making him falter on his feet before shaking it off. Each punch he throws in my direction I dodge and then return with two of mine. I pound into him with a lethal brutality—but he never drops. Each punch to his face earns me more of a twisted grin. Each jab to his center has him laughing.

"You get off on putting your hands on helpless women? Touching *my* goddamn woman? Sticking your dick where it doesn't fucking belong?" I pant, slamming my fist into his body again.

He gets a few good licks after that, my mind torn between finishing him and getting to Emmy. Each second I don't see her move from the corner of my eye is too long.

"She fucking liked it," he goads.

Judging by the look on his face and the fact that his exposed dick is still bobbing around, he is getting off on this fight.

Reaching forward, I grip his dick in my hand and pull hard with a vicious twist—giving it every ounce of strength I have in me. I hear a satisfying pop followed quickly by his howl of agony before he drops to the floor and vomits profusely.

"This is for Emmy, you sick fuck," I howl, bringing my leg

back and kicking him with all my strength in the jaw.

His eyes roll back and he's out cold. Hell, he could be dead for all I know.

I get to Emmy's side and take inventory of her injuries. Her throat has two very angry handprints that are already bruising. Careful not to harm her further, I check her pulse—slow but steady. Her face, chest, and arms have various cuts and bruising. There's a gash on her temple that is bleeding, but it looks to be slowing.

Not wanting to move from her, I wrap the sheet she's lying on around her body and carefully scoop her into my arms. My leg protests against the added weight, but I push through the pain.

There isn't anything that can stop me from saving my angel.

By the time I reach the lobby, the lights of the police cars are starting to bounce off the window. Running in with guns drawn and shouts to freeze is the only thing that keeps me from powering through them.

"Set the woman down and step away," one of them demands.

I shake my head and drop to my knees.

"Put her on the floor, sir, and step away now."

I still don't put her down. I can't. How can they expect me to just drop her on this cold, unforgiving floor?

"I'm not going to tell you again."

I can hear the promise in his tone, but fuck me. They're going to have to have to drag me away.

"Officer! That's not the one. He's the one who told me to call you!" The clerk from earlier yells.

I don't take my eyes off the officer I assume is in control. Not blinking or giving, but showing him that I'm not the one he needs to be worried about. Emmy is.

"She needs a medic badly. She has deep neck lacerations, a possible concussion, and two visibly broken limbs. Pulse was weak but holding steady approximately two minutes ago."

He nods and waves the paramedic through, and only when they place their board down do I release my hold on her.

Not willing to go far, I stand and move out of the way so that they can work on her. Then I look over at the police officer and breathe in deep. I can't be there for Emmy until I make sure that motherfucker can't ever get near her again.

"Sir? The assailant is in room four seventeen. When I left him, I believe he was breathing, pants around his ankles, and I'm pretty sure I broke his dick. My name is Maddox Locke. I'm the technical specialist and head of all surveillance and recon at Corps Security. I'm going to reach into my pants and grab my wallet so I can give you my card. Also, if you would like to call your chief, he can vouch for me. But I'm going to tell you this right now. When they load her up, I'll be in that ambulance. When you need my statement, you can call my cell and I will tell you when I can give it to you. But I will not be leaving my woman's side."

His eyes are wide when I finish talking. The other two officers who had come in with him left the second I gave the room number.

"I've heard about you guys. I'll give him a call, and if he gives me the green light, I'll let you go, but we will need your statement ASAP."

"I hear you."

My eyes are still on Emmy as I reach in my jeans and pull one of my cards out of my wallet. I can hear him talking on the phone and I know from his tone that he's getting chewed out by his chief. The plus side to having people owe you favors. You catch the police chief's wife in bed with another man and you have an instant ally.

"Yes, sir," he says before addressing me. "When we finish here, I'll be in touch. You're free to go when the ambulance is ready."

I nod my head, still not removing my eyes from Emmy. Silently praying that she is going to be okay.

When the adrenaline starts to drop, I feel the severity of the situation fall heavily on me. My eyes prickle, and as I stand there helplessly watching her fight, I cry for the first time since I lost my leg eleven years ago.

# CHAPTER 22
## Maddox

DURING THE twenty-minute drive to the hospital, I don't move my eyes from her face. She still hasn't woken, and even though I'm being told that she is stable, there won't be anything that can soothe my soul until I see those honey-wheat eyes. I need to see that she is going to be okay. They can tell me until they're blue in the face—until my angel comes back to me, I'm not leaving her side.

They stabilize her arm and leg, get her IV set up, and monitor her heart rate on the ride. The whole time, my eyes never leave her face. I can feel the paramedics moving around, checking her vitals, and communicating with the hospital about her condition.

I sit there like a worthless blob and wait.

"Sir, do you require any medical attention?" one of them asks.

I shake my head, not willing to move from my vigil.

"Are you—"

"I'm fine," I stress.

The rest of the trip is a blur. The doors open when we arrive and the nurses work together with the EMT duo to move her into the hospital. When we reach the double doors, I'm stopped with a small hand against my chest. I almost plow right through her on my quest to stay by Emmy's side.

"Sir, you can't go any farther. If you will follow me, I'll take you to the waiting room."

She has to be fucking insane to think I'm going to just let them take Emmy.

"No."

"I'm sorry, but you have no choice. It's hospital policy. I understand you're worried, but your wife is in good hands."

My heart seizes when she calls Emmy my wife, and right when I see the doors close, the severity of the situation crashes into me and I crumble to the floor.

She doesn't move. I can see her stupid, yellow Crocs and I focus on them like a lifeline.

"Is there someone I can call for you, sir?" she whispers, crouching down to give me her kind eyes.

"I need my… I need Emmy," I whimper, the sound so foreign to my ears. My throat is on fire and I have to work double time to stifle the sobs that want to bubble up.

*Man the fuck up, Maddox. Emmy needs you to stay strong.*

She gives me the time I need to get my shit together and then offers her hand to help me stand. I wave her off and stand—or attempt to—before my leg protests my weight and I fall to my knees.

"Fuck!" I exclaim, my outburst echoing through the halls.

A few other staff members look over at me with concern. One steps forward to offer Little Miss Yellow Crocs some help, but she waves him off.

"Are you injured?" Her voice is low, controlled, and clinical. Her worry for my mental stability is clearly being trumped now that physically I'm falling to fucking pieces.

"Old injury that I aggravated," I hedge and go to stand again. I cringe when I try to give my leg some weight. I need to get off of it, get the prosthetic off so whatever damage I did tonight doesn't get worse.

"May I check?"

I shake my head and pull my pant leg up, showing her without words what she needs to know.

She gives me a small smile and a nod. "Come with me. Let's get you off your feet somewhere comfortable until the doctor finishes up with your wife and comes to find you, okay?"

She leads me to a small breakroom of sorts with a couch in the center of the room, some tables and vending machines off to the far corner, and a scattering of lockers on the other.

"I'll let the doctors know where you are so that they can come and fill you in. No one will bother you here, and if you need to make some calls to family, just use the phone on the end table next to the couch. I'll go get some ice and lotion for your stump. No sense in having some macho-man issues when you need to make sure to avoid exasperating your skin further. Do you feel like you need anything else?"

I shake my head, waiting to hear some sort of disgust about my disability, but it never comes.

"Be right back."

I move towards the couch, drop down, and lean my head back. I should be calling everyone—getting them here—but I feel so hopelessly lost that I don't even know which way is up.

I roll up my pants and go through the movements to get the pressure off my stump. When I get my leg off, the skin is slightly irritated and red, but luckily, there aren't any sores. A little ice and

I should be good to go by the time Emmy needs me.

The nurse comes back, gives me a cool gel pack, and hands me some lotion. I rub it liberally on my skin before throwing the cool pack down.

"You seem to have it covered without my help," she laughs.

"Been doing it long enough," I say in a monotone.

"Right. I know you aren't going to listen to me, but you really should keep your weight off it—even if it's just for the night."

"With all due respect—"

"Tracey," she supplies.

"Well, with all due respect, Tracey, I don't really give a flying fuck about my damn stump right now. As soon as I can get to Emmy, the better. She doesn't need to be alone."

She gives me a soft smile, her blue eyes shining with compassion. "I understand. My husband lost his leg in Afghanistan, so I can respect your pride when it comes to your body, sir, but you can check it at the door. You military men are all the same," she laughs, and I narrow my eyes. "It's written all over you, so it wasn't too hard to guess. You know your body better than I do, but I can promise you this—I'm not judging you and no one else will. You should be proud of everything you've overcome and not look at it as such a burden. And before you ask, that's written all over you too."

I don't speak. No need to. I let her words sink in and, for the first time, think of my injury as a badge of what I've overcome. Could she be right?

"I'll let that simmer while I go check on your wife." She pats my thigh and leaves the room.

Some of the ice-cold fear holding me down weakens from just

thinking about Emmy as my wife. When they said it earlier, I didn't do shit to correct them. The thought of her walking down the aisle towards me, her body covered in white lace, her eyes full of love, and that heart-stopping smile all for me does something to me.

It takes that flame of hope—the one I've been feeling for months, afraid I would somehow extinguish the fire if I just allowed myself a second to believe—to flicker a few times before it starts to warm my body with its warm glow.

We're going to get past this. *She* is going to get past this, and I vow to never let a day go by without joining the fight she's been warring on her own for us.

I'll stand by her side until I'm no longer wanted—and then, if that day ever comes, I'll throw her over my shoulder and carry her the rest of the way.

This is my second chance. The time that I man up and take a chance at everything being blessed with her love could bring me.

# CHAPTER 23
## *Maddox*

I MAKE THE only phone call I need to make to ensure that everyone else is notified. By the time I get my shit together long enough to make the call, the sun is starting to climb and I know it won't be long before the officers from last night start trying to find me.

Axel promises to handle getting my cell number switched and a replacement phone to me as soon as possible, knowing that they'll need to get ahold of me and mine is still somewhere in that hotel's halls. I give him the only information I have—that she was stable when we arrived.

I've just dropped the phone down onto the base when the door opens and Tracey walks back in. She gives me a smile, shutting the door softly.

"Can I get some information on your wife? We can wait for the insurance stuff if you don't have it on you, but they need to know some general information."

I nod but don't move my eyes up from their fixed position on the door, willing someone to come and tell me how she is.

I go over the basic information on Emmy. Just talking about her so clinically is making my skin itch. I need to see her. I have to see her.

"Do you know anything?" I question hopefully.

She looks over her shoulder at the door, I assume trying to decide if she should tell me what she knows. "When Dr. Moss comes in, let's pretend we didn't have this conversation. I snuck into the exam room with the ruse of needing some paperwork signed. She had x-rays on her arm and leg. Last I heard, they had set and stabilized both and will cast them when the swelling subsides. She's going to be okay."

"Jesus," I pray. "Anything else? Extent of her other injuries?" My eyes wildly scan her face and my heart pounds rapidly. Goddamn it, I need to get to her.

"I'm sorry," she says and stands. "It shouldn't be much longer."

"Her family is coming. Should I be somewhere else so that they can get to me?"

She nods. "Let's go out to the waiting area. There's a separate room for family that we can have you settle in. They will be able to find you there."

It takes me a second to get everything settled with my leg. The pain is better now that I had the time to get off it. Not a hundred percent, but an immense improvement.

My new 'holding area' isn't small, but once everyone arrives, it will be. I walk over to the windows, stuffing my hands into my pockets, and try to reason with my mind. I feel the almost uncontrollable urge to start bulldozing my way through this building until I'm with her. My demons, now recognizing her for what she is—their blessing—are restless without her soothing soul.

It took me so fucking long. I stole years from her—from us—

because I was too much of a pussy to take a chance. I still worry that I might unwillingly harm her, but I now believe that we need each other on a greater scale.

Regardless of my fears and concerns, the only way I might ever begin to heal is with her walking each step with me.

"Maddox?" I tense when Axel's hand touches my back. "You okay, brother?"

I'd love to punch him in the face, get some of this excess energy out, but I know he isn't asking the ludicrous question for shits and giggles.

"No," I tell him honestly. "But I will be when they let me back there."

"I understand. Here."

I turn and look down at the phone in his hand.

"Called your carrier and had your number transferred over, so if they call, it's all good."

"Appreciate it," I mumble. "Where's Izzy?"

"At home with Nate. She wanted to come with me, but Nate's sitter needed an hour to get there. Melissa is bringing the girls and Cohen over before she and Greg head this way. Everyone else should be here shortly."

I don't respond, choosing to rather turn towards the window and wait. It shouldn't be taking this fucking long.

An hour passes before the room is full of everyone who loves Emmy. All worried. Everyone silent. I'm sure they're afraid to speak at this point, and I honestly don't know what I would do if they did. I'm hanging by a thread that's been unraveling for hours.

My eyes close just before two small arms wrap around me. She doesn't speak—she doesn't need to—and she just offers me her strength. I'm fine until she starts to hum and I remember when our positions were switched and Izzy needed me to be her strength. Her lifeline when her world was crumbling around her. Before she and Axel finally got past their issues and came together again. Fought *their* demons and won.

Her heavy belly brushes against me when I shift and open my arms. She gives me a soft smile and moves her body closer. I take everything she's giving and look across the room where her husband is frowning. Even though I know he's worried just like the rest of us, that frown is because his woman is in my arms.

"Appreciate it, Iz, but maybe you should get back to your husband now?"

She looks over at her grumbling husband and rolls her eyes. "He'll get over it. You need me."

She doesn't let up. Not when Melissa walks over and joins. Not when Dee shuffles under my arm and burrows close to Izzy. And not even when Chelcie brings up the rear and wraps her arms around the three other girls. Each of them at one time was just as lost as I was. I've watched, helped, and cheered silently from the shadows as each of them overcame and thrived with one of my brothers.

Hope. Trust in the unknown. And love. It's been right in front of me for so long, but I've been too blind to see it.

I close my eyes and let my guard down. Then I take the masks and shields I've used as tools to keep others out and throw them away. With a deep shudder, my breath catching and my arms tightening around the each of the women in my life who have loved every dark piece of me, I allow myself to break.

Their arms get tighter, and together, they help me hold myself up. Help me let it out without judgment and give me the time I need to express my pain.

I open my eyes, the wetness falling from my lids and rolling down my cheeks. When I meet each of my brothers' eyes, I see their understanding and support trained my way. All four of them give me a tip of their chins and turn their attention back to each other—allowing me this moment.

Thirty minutes later, the women back next to their husbands—and since Sway walked in during the tail end of their hugs, I just detached him from my body seconds before—the doctor comes into the room.

"The family of Ms. Keeze?" he asks the room.

I move quickly and stand before him. "Maddox. Husband," I say in way of greeting.

He scans the room before addressing me again. "Is there somewhere we can speak privately?"

"This is her family, Doctor, so anything you need to tell me can be said right here."

"Very well. Your wife is resting as comfortably as possible at the moment. X-rays show that she has a fracture to her ulna, and although it's stabilized, the swelling is too great for her to be placed in a cast at the moment. She has also has a transverse tibia fracture. The swelling issue is also present. Both will be placed in a cast as soon as possible. Her throat will be sore for a few days. There isn't any internal damage. However, she was complaining about the pain. I placed two stitches to the laceration on her temple. All things considered, your wife is a very lucky woman."

My mind is racing to make sense of her injuries. I understand, at some level, what he is trying to say to me, but I can't compute it until I see her.

"Do you have any questions for me?"

"I need to see her."

"She's just being moved to her room now. How about we take a walk and we can go over those questions."

I nod and mutely follow behind. He goes over her injuries in more detail and tells me that she will need to be admitted for observation and hopefully her swelling will be down enough for her cast to be placed by morning.

"I understand that you rode in with her, but it's been a few hours and her bruising had gotten a little worse. Be prepared, Mr. Keeze—she isn't going to look like the woman you brought in here. The bruising will fade. The bones will heal. She's alive."

He gives me a moment. I slow my breathing and will my heart to calm before it beats out of my chest. With a shaking hand, I push open her door and step into the room. When I see her battered face for the first time, a deep rumble bursts through my chest. I push it down and focus on being there for her. Hesitantly, I walk forward. Then I take the chair placed on her right side and reach out for her slim hand. Feeling the warmth against my skin is the green light my soul has been waiting for.

I drop my head to the bed, next to her hip, and press my lips to her fingers.

The bed shakes with my heaving breaths. I let it all out, prepared to stuff my pain back inside when she wakes and be the strength *she* now needs.

"I love you," I whisper hoarsely against her skin, closing my eyes tight and vowing to God for the first time in too many years to be the man she deserves.

# CHAPTER 24
## Emmy

I DON'T WANT to move. I keep my eyes closed long after I heard him whisper those three words, their meaning filling my body, effortlessly picking up the pieces of my heart, which I thought would be forever broken.

Turning my head and ignoring the soreness in my neck, I open my eyes. The lighting in the hospital room causes me to blink a few times, the tint on the windows keeping the sunlight from being to harsh, but my dry eyes take a few moments to adjust. My body hurts, but the majority of my pain is coming from my arm and my leg. I know from before the doctor brought me in here that I broke both my left arm and leg. Other than some other minor injuries, I'm fine—all things considered.

Having Maddox here is just the medicine I need. Well, that and the high dose of pain meds they pushed through my IV thirty minutes before. I'm sure my pain level would be quite different had I not gotten those.

Moving my eyes down to where I feel him against my side, I take in his hunched over form. His large frame is folded in the plastic chair, both tan hands wrapped around my much paler one, his head lying against the mattress so that his mouth is resting next to my fingers. His eyes are closed, and if it weren't for the wet tear streaks falling down his cheeks, I wouldn't even think he was awake. Even though he's hurting, he's more at peace in this moment that I've ever seen him.

"Hey," I mumble. My voice is deeper and rougher than normal.

When he hears me speak, he jerks up in his seat—eyes wide and hopeful. "God…"

He doesn't say anything else, so I give him a small smile, trying to let him know that I'm okay.

"Do you need the nurse?"

I shake my head.

"Water?" His brow crinkles, and if he weren't still holding my hand in a death grip, I would run my fingers over them.

Again, I shake my head, causing his frown to deepen.

"Bathroom?"

"Stop, Mad. I'm good. I have everything I need right here next to me," I sigh. It takes me a little while to get the words out—my throat rawer than I thought. "I just need you."

His expression changes—his face going soft as his eyes heat. It's an expression I've never seen from him but always dreamt of.

"I was coming back to you, Em."

"I know." I smile and pull my hand from his grip.

His eyes go wide until he notices that my intent isn't to pull away.

I reach out weakly and run my fingertips along his stubbled cheek. "I like this."

"Do you?" His lips twitch, and I feel the mood lighten.

"I do." I run my fingers along his jaw a few more times before I cup his cheek in my palm, looking deep into his eyes before speaking. “I love you too,” I whisper.

He jumps in his seat. Not much though, and if I hadn’t been studying his reaction, I would have missed it. His eyes search mine for a few beats, the uncertainty clear as day. I give him the time he needs, preparing myself for if he rejects me. This is, in a sense, our moment of truth. His jaw ticks and his deep breathing fills the silence.

I watch his emotions fighting for control, each one playing out in a fascinating display. The fear. Struggle to believe. And the hope that he can. Them, finally, I see them all clear and the acceptance and love take over.

“My sweet angel,” he finally says on a sob.

I watch his face as he crumbles and the tears start to slowly fall. “Come here,” I beg.

He looks at me, lying in a bed that is too narrow for him to join, and appears confused, those tears still falling. I silently signal for him to move forward and he scoots a few inches towards me on his chair. I motion for him to lean over and he does, his face hovering just over the bed. I run my hand from his arm, up his shoulder, then around his neck. His eyes close when my skin makes contact with his, and I pull him towards me until his face is just inches from my own. Two of his hot tears fall and land on my cheeks. His eyes instantly drop to them and watch them fall to the bed.

“Kiss me.” My request brings his eyes—and their heat—back to mine.

When his lips touch mine, I sigh and he takes that in. There isn’t anything sexual about this kiss. This is us becoming one—and it’s every bit as beautiful as I knew it would be.

Two officers come by and take my statement. The whole time, Maddox fumes and growls, and by the time they leave, I'm exhausted. I sleep through our friends checking on me. Then I sleep through lunch and dinner. The doctor comes back early in the evening and takes me to have my casts put on. At this point, I've had enough pain meds flowing through my system that, even though it hurts like a bitch to just move from room to room, I am able to take it.

When we make it back to my room, Maddox is pacing in tight rotations. His hands are clasped behind his neck as his worry fills the room. I know he's having a hard time processing everything that happened, but I don't want him to feel this way. He isn't responsible for what happened—even if a part of me is concerned that he will feel just that.

His eyes snap to the doorway when he hears me and he stands there, giving them space before he's back at my side again.

"You need to get some sleep," I remind him—something I've been saying for the last few hours.

"I'm good."

"And I'm not going anywhere."

Since I'm unwilling to back down and sure that it's written all over my face, he gives me a tight nod.

The nurse comes in a moment later and checks my vitals before going over my pain and thankfully giving me another dose. My eyes start to get heavy shortly after she leaves the room. The dim lighting, now that the sun has gone down, does nothing to help me stay awake.

"Promise me you'll sleep?" I slur.

"Sure, angel."

I try to say something else. Maybe beg him. But my eyes win and I'm fast asleep seconds later.

THE NEXT morning, I'm in a foul mood. Maddox is pushing himself on empty. He won't sleep. His eyes never leave wherever I am. I forced him to eat breakfast this morning, all but shoving it in his mouth myself. His scowl is scaring the staff and I'm about to snap.

"Did the officers tell you what happen with…*him*?" I ask after the doctor leaves the room with the promise that discharge paperwork should be done within the hour.

"Yeah. He's locked the fuck up," he snaps.

"Chill your attitude, Maddox Locke. Don't make me spank the sass right out of you."

His eyes widen slightly just a brief second before he throws his head back and his laughter bellows through the room. I smile at the sound and enjoy this carefree version of him. Until he stops and hits me with his narrowed eyes—hard and serious. He moves closer, careful not to jar the bed, but places both hands on either side of my body and leans in.

"Make no mistake, Emmy. Once I get you home and healed, I'll be spanking that ass until it's bright pink and you're begging for me to make you come. Then I'm going to eat you until you're screaming for me to let you come. When you think you can't take a second more of just the mere thought of the pleasure that I'm going to give you, only then will I think about giving that to you, but it will most definitely be *after* I spank the sass out of *you.*"

He leans back, his ass hitting the chair and his arms crossing over his powerful chest. I gulp. I have nothing for that. No smartass comeback and no witty reply. Absolutely nothing.

"Jesus Christ, you two could make a nun come."

My eyes widen in shock and Maddox just shakes his head, a small smile dancing across his lips. I can't look—knowing that our moment wasn't just for us is pretty freaking embarrassing.

"Cat got your tongue, Em?" Dee laughs.

I turn and watch her push her way past Axel with a shove, followed by a laughing Izzy.

"It was pretty damn hot, girlfriend." Izzy laughs, looking over at Maddox with a wink before throwing her hand up.

He acts like he's annoyed, but I can see the happiness in his eyes. He shuffles to his feet and slaps his hand against hers.

"How are you feeling?" Beck asks, walking into the room and pulling Dee into his chest.

"Pretty good. Sore, but the pain meds are way too good for me to complain." My joke falls short and they all look at me. "What? Do you want me to break in half and cry? I fought because I had a reason to," I snap, looking over at Maddox. "I'm not going to let those jerks have one second of my thoughts. I'm a fighter. A survivor. And you will all do damn well to remember it."

"Well, hell yeah, chick!" Dee yells, earning her a stern look from Beck. "What? You all should know better than to think that our little Emmy wouldn't bounce back."

"There's bouncing back and there is denial," Melissa says sharply from the door.

I can see Greg standing right behind her, his eyes scanning my body from head to toe—his frown matching the ones the others are wearing.

"Would you guys stop? I made a promise to myself a while ago that I wouldn't live in the past. The past I can't control, but the future is all mine. I'm choosing to let this make me a stronger person—to not let it win in any way. One step forward, right, Axel?"

The meaning of my words sinks in and his handsome face breaks out in a huge grin. "Yeah, Em… One step forward and never back. I get you."

"Well *I* don't get her. What the hell are you two talking about?" Dee snaps.

"Clearly someone didn't get their coffee this morning," Izzy mutters under her breath.

"Or maybe someone is hormonal and doesn't understand when her friends speak in some code!" Her eyes go wide and she slaps her hand over her mouth.

All of our eyes go from her to Beck, who is just standing there with one proud-ass grin on his face.

"Well…okay then," Izzy says, hiding her shock. "When did you find out?"

"A few weeks ago. We just haven't had a chance to say anything. Clearly my big mouth doesn't understand that this isn't a good time."

"Oh shut up. This is a great time." Did I really just say that?

"Really? You laid up in the hospital is a great time?" she snaps, folding her arms over her chest.

"You want to pick a fight with me over this? I'm the one in the bed, which means everything I say goes."

"That makes no sense, Em. How much of those drugs do they

have you on?" She moves forward and pokes my IV bag.

"That's not the pain meds, you window licker," Melissa huffs. She walks farther into the room and moves to my right side. The side that Maddox hasn't left since last night. Then she stands next to him and waits. When it becomes clear that he isn't moving, she actually shoos him. Reaches her hand up and waves him off. "Seriously, you overgrown ape. Move so I can see to my girl."

"Not your girl, Melissa. Remember that. I'll give you a second with *my* girl, but only a second." He backs up slightly, giving her just enough room to move in and give me a hug. Well, kind of a hug. More like a pat on my shoulder and a pressing of her cheek against mine.

"You really want to go home with that caveman?" she asks with a huge smile on her stunning face.

"Ah, he's nothing but a big teddy bear," I joke.

"Sass, Emersyn," he scolds.

"Over the top, Maddox," I counter.

He grumbles under his breath but steps back and allows the girls to move closer. As he steps in the corner, the guys walk over to speak with him. I remind myself later to ask him what they're talking about.

The conversation flows around the room. My girls—my family—sitting around me on the sides of the bed. All except for Izzy—a very pregnant Izzy—who is sitting in the chair next to us.

They leave an hour later. Exhausted from all the activity plus having my last dose of pain medication before they release me, I crash hard. I get a good nap in before Maddox wakes me up asking if I'm ready to get out of here.

When we finally make it down to the front of the hospital,

where Maddox's black Charger is waiting for us, my eyes widen when I see the crunched-up front end. Noticing the question before it's even out, he snaps, "Don't ask," before lifting me out of the wheelchair and carefully placing me in the passenger's seat.

"You ready to go home?" he asks after starting the car.

"I am home," I reply with a smile, and then I lay my head back and close my eyes with a smile on my face.

# CHAPTER 25
## Maddox

"I'M GOING to take a shower. You good?"

Emmy looks up at me from where she's resting in the middle of my bed. The bed I carried her to after I refused to bring her to the guest room when she pitched a mammoth fit. Her argument is that we shouldn't rush things. Mine is that we've wasted enough time.

She's also lost her fucking mind if she thinks I'm letting her out of my sight for a good, long while.

"I'm freaking fine," she huffs.

My lips twitch when she tries to throw her attitude around by crossing her chest with her good arm. "It loses a little of its intimidation factor that way."

Her jaw drops and she throws her book at me. I watch it sail across the room and slap me in the chest before tumbling carelessly to the ground.

I keep my feet planted and let my arms hang relaxed at my sides, but there is no mistaking that she sees my impatience written all over my face. It shouldn't be like this—us arguing. She's frustrated with her inability to care for herself and I'm unwilling to bend on anything. Fuck moving too fast. If I hadn't had my head so far up my ass that I could taste the bullshit I was spewing everywhere, then this whole 'moving too fast' bullshit wouldn't be happening.

Last night, while she slept, I let my mind wander to where we would be had I given in to the drug that is Emmy's love. I let myself picture a future I never thought I would see. Blessings. That's all I saw. A wife, maybe some kids, and more happiness than I imagined possible.

Those are the things I'm fighting for now, and Jesus, I'm not exactly the one to beat around the bush when there is something I want. No, something I need.

"You really want to toss that sass around? It's adding up, baby, and I can't fucking wait."

Her eyes widen and her mouth moves silently.

"Nothing to say?" I ask as I step toward the bed. "I get it, Em. I've given you every single reason to doubt me. I've driven that into you and I'm sorry." I sit on the bed, shift so that I have one hand planted next to her hip, and bring the other up to cup her face, leaning in close enough that our noses touch and our breath mixes together. "I'm here. I'm not going anywhere and I'm fighting—for you, for me, for us. Don't give up on me because I took too long."

Her breathing accelerates. I study her face, noticing with great satisfaction that her pulse is going insane. The vein in her neck is pulsing faster with each passing second.

"It's not that I'm giving up on you—or us—Maddox. I just think that we need to talk about things before we jump into bed with each other."

"I'm not going to fuck you," I say. Her eyes narrow at that, and I could kick my own ass for blurting that out. "Yeah, clearly I'm not good at this shit, Em. Cut me some slack. Bottom line, I don't want you away from me. I *need* you near me. I need to feel your warm skin, smell your intoxicating scent, and hear your sass even when you're silent. I get that we need to hash shit out, but right now, I need to feel that you're still here more than I need to waste time with some pleasantries of separate bedrooms. I need you, Em. Maybe even more than you need me at the moment, and that's a whole fucking lot." I kiss her lightly, breathing her scent in deeply, before taking off to the bathroom to shower.

## Emmy

"OKAY, OKAY. Get your wits about you, girlfriend," I mumble to myself.

I can hear him moving around in the bathroom, the door cracked I'm sure so he can hear me if I need him. He's humming to himself, the almost upbeat tune so unlike him. I've witnessed the closed-off, hard-around-the-edges, vibrating-with-anger Maddox slowly start to fade away since our time at the cabin. It's hard to pinpoint when I noticed it happen first. But I do remember the exact moment he flipped a switch and the old Maddox came back.

So, yeah—I'm a little hesitant to believe that this is real. I would be stupid not to have my doubts. I also want nothing more than to knock all this stress off my shoulders and *believe*. I was so ready to just give it all up. To give him up.

*If you don't take this opportunity, this second chance, you'll regret it forever. Just put one foot in front of the other. Baby steps...*

*We all have to learn to walk somewhere, right? And then—then, when you get steady on your feet—that's when you gallop with everything you have. The beauty of it all will be that the man by your side has already learned how to walk again once, so he'll be there—ready— to hold your hand the whole way.*

I repeat that over and over. Clearly lost in my head, I missed Maddox walking back into the room. He's standing next to his ridiculously huge bed, a towel hanging low on his hips and water drops still rolling down his chest. I watch as one drops from his chin and lands between his pecs. My hand twitches in my lap as I watch it slowly—so erotically slowly—travel through the dusting of black hair, between the two perfectly sculpted rows of his abs, and then continue its path right between the deep V disappearing between his white towel.

I gulp, the sound so loud that it's like a gunshot blast. At the risk of making myself look like some leacher, I move my eyes back up his torso, shifting the best I can to relieve some of the uncomfortable pressure building between my legs. His tattoos are so vibrant, the red dancing with the black from his wrist to the base of his neck. His chest is bare of ink, but I can see some more red shading on his left side. God, he is delicious.

"You done yet?"

My head snaps up, meeting his laughing eyes. His face completely relaxed and I gasp at his beauty.

Then I stupidly tell him, "You're so beautiful." My cheeks heat instantly.

His lips move, a small twitch, but he doesn't smile. His eyes, however, are bright. The normal hardness has been replaced with contentment.

*He's happy.*

"I'm not sure that's going to do much for my ego," he laughs.

"You're happy?"

Cue the verbal vomit. It has to be my medication.

"I'm getting there, angel."

I nod and his lips twitch again. I watch, stunned, as he turns and drops his towel before walking into the closet.

*Well, fuck me.*

# CHAPTER 26
## *Emmy*

MADDOX CONTINUED to stick close to me as the day faded into night. I slept off and on, the pain and general uncomfortableness of my two broken limbs making it challenging to fall asleep completely. So, naturally, I woke up in a pissy mood. He takes it in stride. And by in stride, I mean he ignores it completely, choosing instead to decide when I need to do certain things.

He forces me to eat dinner by sitting on the side of the bed and holding the fork of chicken to my mouth until I finally give in. Then he decides that I need to use the bathroom, so he carefully carries me into the bathroom, past the huge bathtub and shower area, and into a smaller room just with the toilet. He is kind enough to leave the room for me to have some privacy, but he still leaves the door open.

I lift up on my ass and pull the hem of my shirt so I'm not sitting on it. The embarrassment of my situation makes me cringe. I know he can hear me relieving myself and I hate being this…weak and out of control.

After wiping, I use the wall to stand and then weakly call out, "I'm done."

He comes in scowling because I'm standing. Then he bends to lift me in his arms.

"Is my weight too much?" I ask, worried about his leg.

I admit that I've known about his amputation for years, known it happened long before I came into the picture, but I know nothing else. The outsider would never know. He doesn't limp. He stands tall and proud. He is always wearing pants; I've never seen him with anything other than pants. Even when he goes to the gym I know that he wears long sweats then too.

"You weigh next to nothing, Em. But even if you didn't, I'm good. I've had a long time to get my body to where it is now. Most days, I don't even notice it."

"Really?" I ask when he gently places me down on the mattress. I use my good arm and my hips to shift my body until I get comfortable.

He doesn't say anything. He just stands there and helps me when I need it, placing a pillow back under my leg, rolling the covers back up to my waist, and setting my book back at my side. I let him fuss. It seems to be helping whatever residual issues he's dealing with from yesterday—*the attack.*

Thinking that, once he gets me settled, he will answer me, I'm shocked stupid when he walks out of the room.

Goddamn it. Just when I felt like he was letting me in.

I silently stew in my snit and wait for him to come back so I can *throw my sass* in his face. I hear him moving around farther in the apartment, assuming since it's going on ten at night that he is locking up and shutting everything off. I hear the alarm beep and watch as the keypad next to his bedroom door lights up a few times. I know he has some top-dollar program wired into his place.

The touchscreen alone makes my head hurt.

My frustration builds when he still doesn't come back. I wait, listening to him thump around in another room. I can hear things being moved around, but as much as I try, I still can't place the sound.

When I see him walk through the doorway, I'm ready to go all hurt, pissed-off, and sexually frustrated crazy chick on his ass, but when I see him carrying a medium-sized shoebox, I snap my mouth shut and try to calm myself down.

"I imagine, had I walked back in here empty-handed, that you would have been breathing fire in my direction." Obviously not a question since he doesn't let me respond before continuing. "I meant what I said the other day, Em. I'm ready. To let you in. And I'm ready to fight to be worthy of you. In order for me to do that, I need to accept that you *want* me to let you in—regardless of how much it kills me to show you all the monsters that live inside me. Each and every one of them can be found in this godforsaken box, and I think, at this point, that it will help more than hurt for you to see where I've been coming from. This is that baggage you wanted to help me carry, Em."

When he places the box on my lap, I'm almost afraid to open the top. But afraid or not, this is the moment I've been praying for. The moment when we take another one of our baby steps… together.

His face is soft but slightly worried. My apprehension grows, but I know that, if I don't take this step, we will never move forward. I also know how hard this is for him, and if I reject this simple act, then he might never open up again.

"Okay, baby," I whisper and watch as his body visibly feels

the impact of those hushed word.

He sits on the corner of the bed, next to my hip, and faces me. The box light is against my lap. I search his eyes a few more beats before I lift the lid. I'm not sure what I anticipated, but a box with random papers and trinkets definitely wasn't it.

"What—"

"Right. Besides the fact that all of this is worthless junk, to me, it's a reminder of everything I've failed, harmed, or basically touched and fucked up. A physical reminder—something tangible—to remind me what happens when I believe that monsters aren't real. I can't tell you how many times I would come home from denying us—this—and dug this box out. *This* pile of shit is my pain, the baggage of burdens and ruined pasts that I carry deep within me. I could throw it out tomorrow, but, Emmy, this stuff will always be a part of me."

My heart breaks for him. His pain has always been so obvious. The fact that he holds it even deeper than I ever imagined scares me to death.

"Is this…" I start, picking up the medal thrown carelessly in this mess of junk. If this is what I think it is, there is no way it belongs in here.

He reaches out and gently takes it from my grasp. "Medal of Honor. I never felt like I deserved this—part of the reason that it's in here—but it also didn't seem fair that I came home with this token of valor when it's my fault that two men didn't make it home alive."

"Can I ask how you came to receive this when you claim you aren't worthy of it?"

His eyes never leave the bronze medal resting between his

fingertips. He strokes it almost reverently before speaking, "After the explosion, I was the only one of the three of us still conscious. Badly injured, but I was the only chance we had. I'm not going to go into the details. It really isn't something I want to go over, but it was bad—real bad. I don't remember much of it, but when the nightmares come, I'm right back there—dragging my brothers under our enemy's fire while my body slowly gives up—until we're finally picked up. I lost my leg that day and two families lost damn good men."

"I can't even fathom how that equals unworthiness in your eyes, baby," I whisper and reach out with my good hand to clasp his arm. "Look at me," I demand.

He turns his head. His eyes are troubled, but he looks right at me.

"You're a hero, Maddox. You were then and you continued to be even when you didn't believe it yourself. You made sure that their families had their loved ones home and you did that by putting aside your own personal welfare. You could have left them there and gotten out safely, but you didn't. You went above and beyond."

"I'm not worthy, Em, because it never would have happened if my head hadn't been swimming under the shitstorm I'd left brewing at home."

I take a deep breath before speaking; trying to figure out how to express what I feel in a way that he'll believe me. "Do you honestly believe that?" He nods. "I believe that you do and I hate that. I have no doubt in my mind that, if you looked back now with a clear mind, you would see that, even if you'd been your best that day, you still could have missed something. Baby, you don't deserve this burden. I understand that you need someone to blame, but place that on the people who placed the bomb that triggered this all. Do you think every soldier who goes into the battle zone has no stress, no worry, and no distractions? I highly doubt that. You were the sole survivor of a terrible, tragic accident, but you survived. Be proud that you were able to overcome and get your men home."

"I-I don't know if I can do that."

"Well, then, I just have to help you." I give him a small smile and squeeze his arm. "Do you want to keep going?"

When he nods, I return it with my own before bringing my attention back to the box.

The next item I pick up is a letter, and after reading it, my blood is boiling. I understand grief. I've watched it up close and personal within our group, but what I don't understand is using that grief to lash out at those who do not deserve it.

"Good God, Maddox. I'm not going to argue with you. You have believed this for so long, but let me tell you this much. She was hurting, baby. She needed someone to blame, and just like you blame yourself for something that is unjust, so does she. She took the blame out on the only person who made sense to her. I honestly believe that she regrets each of these words now."

He doesn't try to argue with me. He's going to believe it, but I'm going to keep working on him until he understands just how wrong he is.

The more items we go through, the more I look at him in shock as I try to make sense of it all. From the outside, it's so easy for me to see how wrong he is, but I can't wrap my head around it. Not until we get to the bottom.

There, I see a picture of a much younger, happier, Maddox, tattoos missing from his body. He's standing tall with a big smile on his face. And in his arms is a stunning blonde. From just this picture alone, I can see the evil in her eyes. I don't have to know her personally to know that she's rotten to the core.

"That is Mercedes. I had just asked her to marry me before I left. I was young and dumb, blinded by the thought of a pure love. I spent my whole life wishing for just one person who would love me for me, so when she entered my life, I grabbed on and didn't let go."

"What happened?" I ask, not sure that I want to know the answer to that question.

"My mother happened. Well, to be honest, I think it was a fair mix of my mother, brother, and the power that came behind the Locke name. Something I wasn't interested in then and I still have no interest in now. I wanted a life away from them, and even though I couldn't give everything, I foolishly thought that she would be happy with just me."

He goes on to tell me a tale so twisted that it sounds like he pulled it right off the Lifetime Movie Network. He touched on this back when we were at the cabin, but to hear his life up until he became the version of himself I see in front of me now in so much detail is almost too much.

I want to cry for him, hold him, fix him, but standing in the frontline of all those feelings is the rage I feel for three sorry sons of bitches somewhere in the middle of Texas.

# CHAPTER 27
## Maddox

WHAT I wouldn't give to be inside her head right now. I expected her disgust when I laid all of my pain on her lap—literally—but I never anticipated her anger *for* me to become a force to be reckoned with.

"I hate them," she forces through her clenched jaw. "God…" She shakes her head but doesn't finish.

"Hating them doesn't do anything, Em. Trust me. I've been doing it for so long that I should know."

Her gaze burns into my skin as I pack up the box and close the lid. When I go to remove it from her lap, she stops me by slamming her palm down on the top.

"Don't you dare. We're going to keep this out, and each day, we will come back to it. We can pull them out one at a time, all at once, or just look at the fucking thing for all I care—but one thing we will be doing is talking about this. I'll talk until I'm blue in the face and you're going to sit there and listen to me. And, Maddox?"

"Yes, Emersyn," I respond, waiting to see where she's going with this.

"I don't care if it takes every day I have left on this Earth, but by the time we finish, you're going to be able to let go of everything that's physically in this box and every piece of garbage you've let it collect within you."

By the time she finishes, we're both breathing heavily. I have no doubt that she means it, and even though I can't help but feel nervous about the thought of reliving my nightmares daily, with her, part of me feels instant relief that she isn't giving up on me now that she knows what a vile soul I have.

"I mean it, Maddox."

"I know you do, angel."

"And when we're done, I'm going to remind you of this moment and the promise I'm about to make to you," she says, her eyes begging me to believe.

"Go on," I urge.

"One day soon, when we're able to take the majority of this and throw it away. The day that you believe every word that I'm telling you as the truth that it is—that day, you're going to feel the beauty of life, and the peace that you feel won't even hold a candle to the love I'm going to drown you in."

I give her a nod, not trusting myself to speak, and go to pick up the box again. She doesn't move her hand until I bring my eyes back to hers.

"Don't make me spank that doubt out of you," she teases.

"Emersyn," I warn.

Her eyes spark and her full lips tip up. "Keep doubting me. I dare you."

"That sass is going to get you in trouble soon."

She lets her hold on the box go and smiles. "I'm looking forward to it."

I drop the box on the top of my dresser, turning to look at her so that she sees that I'm willing to do this her way. I would be lying to myself if I said that I'm not hoping she's right. Just the thought of feeling some peace is tempting enough for me to continue this fight. One that I know will be undoubtedly easier as long as she's right there with me.

When I turn around, she's lying on her back and looking at me hopefully. With a deep breath, I round the bed and sit. She's seen me without my leg on. She's seen my stump. She knows what I've been so careful to keep hidden because of the shame it gives me. Even with all of that, she's still here, still wanting to be here. Knowing how I became this broken man didn't change her mind at all.

That doesn't lessen my self-consciousness about my…defect.

"Take it off, baby," she whispers.

"Just give me a second."

"I won't give you a second. I gave you four years' worth of seconds. It's time for you to be a big boy and *take it off*," she fumes.

I look at her and want to laugh at the situation. I should have known that, while I'm falling back on to my own faults and shortcomings, she would still throw her sass. She's broken herself and still stands tall.

Can it really be that easy? To look at my life, find the positives—those things she thinks I'm missing because I'm too busy looking for the bad—and just let go?

*Now or never, Maddox. You either keep moving forward with the hope or you let the fear consume you.*

I hold her eyes, stand, and drop my sweats. Her eyes widen slightly, and had I not been staring at her directly, I wouldn't have seen it. She stands her ground and doesn't even flinch when I drop back down and remove my prosthetic. She doesn't say a thing as I slide back and swing my legs over. She doesn't make a sound until I lift my arm to pull her towards me.

Even then she doesn't say anything with her words. She lets out a shocked gasp and lifts up as best she can with one arm.

"What…" She doesn't finish her question, the words trailing off as she reaches one of her small hands towards my heated skin.

When I feel her fingertips graze the side of my body, I close my eyes and relish in the chills her touch elicits.

"I don't… Is that…Maddox?" Her fingers don't stop their tracing, their searching, as the question she didn't speak lingers in the air.

"Yeah. It's a rose, Emmy. It's a rose that I got the day after I almost gave in and gave myself to you after Axel and Izzy got married."

Her eyes jump to mine, shocked.

"I didn't forget that," I tell her. "Not for a second. Those stolen moments with you in my arms drove two things home—that you will forever be *my* Emersyn Rose and the only place you belonged was in my heart. I couldn't give that to you then, so I did the second best thing. I had a symbol of you placed on my body permanently."

"I don't know what to say to that," she sighs after a few moments of silently searching my eyes.

"So don't say anything. It's there. It happened."

"It's beautiful," she says, looking at the rose that starts just directly under my armpit and ends about six inches down. The rose is bright red, the stem done in black—with her name scripted down its length.

"Yeah…it really is," I agree, not talking about the ink on my body, but the feeling of having her after so long of believing I couldn't.

Maybe she's right. Maybe it is just as simple as she believes. God, I hope so, because if just the thought of her love feels this good, I can't imagine how it will truly feel.

I am just falling asleep, Emmy's body curled as best as she can into me without jarring her arm and leg and her head resting on my outstretched arm. She's been having a hard time sleeping today, so I'm hoping that, by keeping her close, she can rest more easily. A few times she woke up during the day crying out and I know she's thinking about her attack.

It makes me go instantly savage. Like an untamed beast, I want to go on attack mode, but I stifle it down and focus on being there when she needs me. It wouldn't do her a bit of good for me to lash out on her because I'm feeling the terror of having almost lost her.

"Maddox?" she utters into the darkness.

"Emersyn," I rumble back, my voice thick.

"I knew you would save me."

My body jolts and she moans in pain when I jar her body slightly. Shit.

"I fought him because I knew you would come. I fought him because I had a reason not to give up."

I'm shocked stupid, unable to even form a grunt in response because of the feeling of my heart beating wildly as it grows to improbable levels.

"I used everything I had to make sure we would have our chance. I told you I would never stop fighting for you, and even though I was physically fighting for myself, I was in that battle to win not just my life…but yours too.

"Jesus," I gasp past the lump in my throat.

"I would do it all over again. I'll never stop fighting."

I turn so that I'm on my side and shift my arm under her head so that she's resting on the crook of my elbow, coming up off the mattress to cup her cheek with my other hand and bring my face close. Our noses touch first and I rub hers softly before taking her lips in a slow and powerful kiss.

The second my mouth opens, our tongues come together, tangling slowly in a caress so electric that I can feel it burning its power throughout my body. My cock presses against her hip, painfully swollen, and my balls throb with need. My skin burns. I give her everything I have with just our mouths fused together.

I pull back with a gasp when I feel the coiling in the base of my spine warning me that, if I continue, I'm going to embarrass myself.

"Holy crap," she whispers in awe.

"I'm going to be worthy of you, Emmy," I vow softly, my cheek pressed against hers and my lips whispering my promise in her ear. "I promise you, angel. I'm going to be the man you deserve. I—God—I fucking love you."

She lets out a soft puff of air that lightly strokes against my cheek. I feel her chest shaking, and I bet she will be seconds from crying if I lean back.

"Such a poet," she sighs with a slight wobble in her voice. "I've dreamt of hearing you say that, and I should have known that I would get a Maddox Locke version. Well, I *fucking* love you back."

I laugh, kiss her cheek, and move to lie back down. "Are you doing okay with everything that happened, Em?" I ask, afraid of what she will say. I hate the thought of her being fearful of anything.

"Yeah," she breathes. "Yeah, I really am. I could let it put a scar on my mind, but I'm not going to. I didn't fight to live so that I could be scared for the rest of my days. Of course I'm hurt, and I would be lying if I didn't admit that the majority of that hurt isn't the physical reminders—those will heal. It's the thought that my own father sent that monster after me. I guess, like a silly little girl, I had believed that, one day, he would love me like a parent should love their child." She laughs without humor. "I don't want to give them the power over my future, Maddox, so I'm choosing to live for the blessings I have and heal from this."

We don't say anything else, both of us lost in our own thoughts. I replay her words over and over again. Everything she said could be used in my situation. I can continue as I always have—or I can choose to live for the blessings I have resting in my arms.

I want those blessings. I want that blessed life. I want to *live*.

# CHAPTER 28
## Emmy

### Two Months Later

TODAY IS the day! I get my arm cast removed and the cast on my leg switched from the long-leg one to one that stops below the knee. I don't think I could be more excited about this if I were getting a million-dollar bonus and a happy ending. Although, I'm guessing I'll get that happy ending when we get home from the doctor's office. Dr. Moss told us that, depending on his examination, I would most likely be given permission to start weight-bearing activities. Just the thought of being able to get around just a fraction has my spirits soaring.

I've hated that Maddox has basically had to put his life on hold. There hasn't been anything I can do on my own. The only plus is that the sponge baths have become really creative.

Things have changed drastically since that night we whispered our love in the dark. He tells me, even if it isn't daily, that he loves me. He's more open with his thoughts and feelings, but his smiles still come few and far between.

We've also been able to throw away almost all of the contents of his box. There are three things still in there: the letter from his fallen soldier's widow, the picture of that vile bitch Mercedes, and his Medal of Honor. He's also been working with a psychologist to help him further than I can with what pains him. Every day, I see the weight on his shoulders ease up more and more.

I couldn't be prouder of him.

"Are you excited?" he asks, bringing my hand up to his lips for a kiss.

"Hell yeah I am! I'm going to have BOTH my hands now. More for me to rub all over your hard body," I laugh. When his groan echoes through the exam room, my laughter becomes all-consuming. I'm pretty sure I snort too. "Well, and I'll be able to walk to the bathroom on my own. I'm going to miss my sponge baths though."

"You're going to miss your sponge baths? Just last night you were telling me that you hated them and couldn't wait until you had a real bath." His brow cocks, reminding me of the fit I threw last night.

"Uh, yeah…that was before you made me come on your tongue. Hey, I rhymed!" I start to laugh again, leaning back on the elevated exam table and resting my head against the soft padding "Jesus, did you spike my breakfast with something?" I joke, wiping the tears from my eyes and looking over at him.

I sober instantly when I see his face.

"Holy shit," I gasp.

He doesn't flinch. If anything, his smile gets even bigger. I've seen him smile before, but it's never been this big. This beautiful. This… It's everything I've imagined. His whole face changes. His eyes crinkle in the corners, his white teeth in contrast to the golden bronze of his skin, his dark eyes full of pure fucking happiness.

He laughs when I continue to stare at him. I'm afraid to move or speak for fear that it will vanish and I'll never see it again.

"You're beautiful." The whisper slips past my lips without permission and I slap my hand over my mouth with eyes wide.

"Still not sure that's a description I want to own," he grumbles, still smiling.

"Tough shit, big guy. You're stunning."

"Sass, Em."

"Sass, my ass," I tease.

"It's going to be your ass. I have eight weeks of your sass throwing to pink your ass with." He leans in, his arms braced against the table, his face inches from mine, and whispers, "You're going to beg for it. I'm going to enjoy every damn second of it too."

Before I can respond to his delicious threat, the door opens and Dr. Moss walks in. I shift in my seat and give Maddox a narrowed-eyed glare. He laughs and kisses me softly before moving out of the way.

"Are you ready to get started, Emersyn?" the doctor asks.

Without moving my eyes from Maddox, I reply, "You bet your ass I am."

Maddox's deep laughter booms through the small room, and I smile shyly in return. Dr. Moss looks up, trying to figure out what is going on, but he shrugs his shoulder before starting his examination.

Two hours later, we're back in Maddox's repaired Charger and rushing home. He runs two red lights and has us back in half the time.

Tonight is going to be magnificent.

When we park in the garage of the apartment complex, I look over to see Maddox deep in thought, staring out the windshield. He doesn't look troubled, just contemplative.

"You okay over there?" I probe, reaching out and rubbing his thigh with my newly freed arm. It hurts to move my wrist too much. The doctor warned that I would be feeling that way for a while, but I'm confident that, with the therapy plan he's worked out, I'll be back to normal in no time.

"You have no idea the strength it's taking me not to take you now…roughly. I'm worried that I won't be able to hold back and your body isn't ready to be fucked the way I want—no, need—to fuck you. I'm fighting with myself, Em, because right now, if I get out of this car without curbing some of this shit, I'm going to take you harder than you can take."

"Jesus Jones, Maddox. Is that supposed to be a deterrent?"

"You bet your ass it is! You have no idea the things I want to do to you."

"Well, then, I'll tell you what. How about you sit here and think about all those dirty things you want to do to me since you apparently have no plans on actually *doing* them any time soon. Don't mind me. I'll just sit here and take care of myself!"

I'm frustrated. So freaking frustrated. I get where he's coming from, but holy shit! How can he say that stuff and not think it's going to make me need him more?

His nostrils flare and his jaw ticks, but he doesn't move. I huff and jerk my hand from his thigh. The hell with this. I shove my strong hand down my sweatpants, moaning when my fingertips brush over my swollen nub. My panties are soaked, like completely saturated with my desire, and it won't take me but a second to bring myself to completion.

"Emersyn," he warns.

I roll my eyes, flip my fingers under the band on my panties, and push them deep, without ceremony, into my hot core. I can smell my arousal taking over the interior of his car. There is no damn way he can miss it. When I curl my fingers slightly and brush over my sweet spot, I cry out hoarsely, ending it in a long moan. My wetness coats my fingers as my walls starting to tremble. Just a few more thrusts and I'll break into a million pieces. I can feel it building, and even at my own hands, I know it will be powerful.

"Fuck!" His deep voice vibrates through the confined space and my core clenches. "Goddamn it!"

Lost in myself—literally—I don't even see him move before my hand is snatched out of my pants and my fingers are being shoved into his mouth. His tongue swirls around my digits and he closes his eyes on a moan.

He doesn't open them until I feel like my two fingers have been sucked clean. Releasing them with a pop, he gives me his eyes—his black eyes full of fire—and rumbles out a feral growl.

"The next time you try to make yourself come, I'm going to fucking tie you to the bed and tease you until you pass out, but I won't let you come for goddamn hours. I'll bring your body to the edge, primed and ready to fall over the ledge, but never let you fall. Over and fucking over. Your screams of pleasure never hitting the peak that you pray I'll give. I'm in charge of your pussy, Emersyn. Don't fucking forget that your sweetness will only be given by me. My fucking fingers. My mouth. And *MY* cock."

"Holy shit," I pant.

He climbs out of the car, slamming the door behind him, and

walks powerfully to my door. My eyes don't once move from the seat he just vacated.

I'm in his arms a second later, and wordlessly, he's charging to the elevators. For a brief second, I wonder if I pressed him too far before I push his aside and let the thrilling sensation his promise gives me take over.

# CHAPTER 29

## *Emmy*

"YOU NEED help stripping, Em?" he asks me when he sets me down on the edge of his bed.

I shake my head, not really sure if I'm answering him or telling myself. I honestly have no idea if I'll be able to get my clothes off.

"That's what I thought." His hands go to the hem of my tee and swiftly pull it over. My bra comes off even faster. Placing his hands under my armpits, he lifts my ass off the mattress. "You good?" he asks, making sure I have my balance before continuing.

With my nod, his hands go to the elastic band at the top of my baggy sweats. He's more careful with my pants, moving down as he pulls them and my panties to the ground. I feel his lips press against my knee and travel up my leg.

And just like that, he's gone. I sway, but his strong arms grab my shoulders to help steady me. After making sure I'm good on my feet, he takes a step back before lifting his shirt over his head. Inch by delectable inch, his stomach comes into view first. His wide chest is next. Then I bring my eyes to his and lick my lips. His focus follows the path of my tongue, and I have to squeeze my thighs tight when his groan rumbles through the room.

I bring my hands to my breasts and caress the swollen skin. My weaker arm gives me some pain when I tweak my nipples, but the look on his face makes it one hundred percent worth it.

"Emersyn," he growls, palming his crotch.

"Maddox," I counter.

And just like that—he attacks.

My body is hauled off the floor when his hands return under my arms and lift. Then his mouth takes mine in a hungry kiss full of possession. I bring my legs up and wrap them around his waist, moaning deeply into his mouth. His hands flex against my ass, his hard cock rubbing against my seeping core. I toss my head back when he pulls one large hand off my ass before bringing it back—hard—in a biting slap.

"More," I beg.

"With fucking pleasure, Emmy."

He sets me back on the mattress and steps back. I watch as his hands go back to his pants, pulling his belt off slowly—calculating—and dropping his pants. He doesn't even move to take them off all the way. I know it will take longer with his prosthetic still on than he's willing to take. His rock-hard cock springs out, the head purple and angry, the loop through the tip wet with his come. I reach out and brush my hand against his thigh, cup his balls, and then tease his length with my touch. The feeling of his ladder against my skin makes me shiver in anticipation.

"Hands off and roll on to your stomach, Emersyn."

I immediately remove my hand, craving the promise his words provoke.

It takes me a second, my arm still too weak to help my movements, my leg—still in the cast—a big annoyance. He gives me the time I need, and when I'm situated and look back at him, he's stroking his cock behind me. His eyes are heavy, his face flushed.

I did this to him.

"You still want it hard? Want me to take your body as roughly as I can without hurting you?"

"God, yes!"

His hand slaps down on my ass with a loud crack. "Fucking beg me, Emersyn."

With pleasure. "Please, Maddox. Please take my pussy hard. Give me your cock and take my body with everything you have."

His hand comes down on the other cheek, the sting making me cry out in pleasure. "Again," he demands.

"Please, Maddox, baby. Take me. Make me come on your cock until my come is dripping from my body."

His palm comes down on a different spot, smoothing the burn with his palm before challenging, "Again."

"God damn! FUCK ME!" I scream.

"That's my girl," he growls.

His hand comes down seven more times, each a new location, and his palm rubs the sting out after each one. My breath is coming so rapidly that I'm starting to think I really might pass out like he threatened earlier.

Right when I think I can't take a second more, he helps me flip over and grabs my hips, pulling me until my ass is all but hanging off the bed. I look down and notice that the height of his bed puts my pussy level with his hips. His cock aligns perfectly with my waiting body.

"Not fucking you with a condom, baby. I know you're clean. You know I'm clean. And I'll be damned if there is anything between us."

"No condom. Just fuck me!" I scream when he starts rubbing his cock's head against my center. Each time the metal of his piercing hits my throbbing clit, I scream again. By the time he finally pushes in, I'm crying.

His balls slap against my ass with the force of his thrust. I bring one hand up and grab his forearm where he's holding my hips, my nails digging in. I shout loudly when I start to come. He grunts as his movements become uncoordinated.

He pushes in deep and doesn't move, his chest heaving and his eyes closed tight. I wiggle, trying to get him to move again, but his fingers on my hips dig in and his eyes snap open.

"Don't fucking move. I'm not going to come in thirty seconds like some teenage shit."

"You have to move. God, baby, I can feel every inch of you stretching me wide."

With a grumble, he pulls out a few inches—enough for me to feel his piercings rubbing against my inner walls. When he pushes forward, I feel him hitting even deeper than before.

I pant, beg, and scream for him to move, but he just stands there, breathing roughly and flexing his hips.

When I can't take it any longer, I rock against him. If he won't give me what I need, then I'll just fucking take it.

"You think you can make yourself come *ON* my dick? Baby, that's the same thing as using your hands. I make you come. Don't fucking forget it."

He pulls almost all the way out before slamming home. Over and over again, he slams roughly into my body. One hand comes off my hips and his thick fingers rub over my clit, teasing me, before he pinches it between his fingers.

On a hiss, I come again, my juices rushing against his rigid flesh. He gives me one hard plunge into my body before throwing his head back and roaring.

Fucking roaring.

The sound of his release making my orgasm roll on and on to the point where I do, in fact, pass out.

# CHAPTER 30
## *Maddox*

JESUS FUCKING Christ.

I don't think I've come that hard in my life. The feeling of her pussy milking my orgasm from my body was like nothing I've ever felt before.

I look down my body to where I'm still planted deep within her warm heat. I can feel our combined releases running down my balls, and my spent cock twitches to life inside her. It takes everything in me to pry my hands from her hips and pull free of her body. My cock is already starting to beg for more of her sweet cunt.

She doesn't flinch. Not when I release my hold on her hips. Not when I step away from her body—my eyes zeroed in on my cock pulling free. I can see her cream coating me and damned if it doesn't pump my craving for her up to uncontrollable levels. When the head of my cock leaves her heat, causing a slow rush of our mixed come to leak from her, I have to grab on to the mattress from the head rush it gives me.

Never has sex felt like that. I can't even deny that it was that intense because of the feelings we have together.

Not even bothering to dress, I move her slack body so that her head is resting on her pillow. Covering her naked body is the last thing I want, but I have a few things I need to take care of before I can climb into bed with her.

Things that I'm finally ready to let go of, thanks to Emmy, and things I want settled before I take her again.

Over the last two months, I feel like I've changed as a person. I no longer look at the world thinking that, at any given moment, I will destroy those around me. I look at our close group of friends, people I've known for years now, and see that, by knowing me, they haven't felt my demons. They haven't been touched—or *tainted*—by my dark soul. If anything, I can now see the role I've played in helping each one of them come together.

That one took a little longer for me to wrap my mind around. Years of thinking one way was warring against the very real truth that I was wrong.

Or, more importantly, that every fucked-up thing my mother had drilled into my head—making me believe without a doubt—was in fact the catalyst in it all. Her hate for me fueled my own self-hate. I carried it around. I owned it. I let her do that to me.

I refuse to let her have that power over me now. I'm worth more than a lifetime of being alone and afraid of myself.

I'm worth Emmy.

It hasn't been easy these last two months, but it has been rewarding. With the help of both Emmy and the doctor I have been seeing a few times a week, I'm ready. Ready to move on and forward. All those baby steps I've taken with her at my side have paid off and I feel like we can now run a marathon together.

It's one fucking amazing high to feel the love of another. To have her wrap that love around me, refusing to let go, and never waver. Indescribable.

Now, it's time to take the rest of my so-called monsters and toss them where they belong—in the darkest pits of fucking hell.

After making sure Emmy is situated, I laugh when she still doesn't flinch. I knew she was running on some kind of manic high today with the thought of having the use of her arm again. Even the thought of the physical therapy left to build her strength back up hasn't weakened her happiness. Being able to move forward and start bearing weight on her leg was even better. It's going to be harder since her wrist is too weak to support crutches for now, but she can move around now, and that is the important thing to her.

I make the walk over to my dresser and feel my lips twitch when I realize that, for the first time in weeks, I don't feel the dread of what I'm about to do.

Open that fucking box.

It's time.

We've slowly been removing items together, just as she promised, but this part needs to be done by me alone. I need to know that I *can* do this one alone.

Popping the lid, I take in the three remaining items. The question is: Which one do I take care of first?

I grab the letter from Johnson's widow first. One of the hardest things for me to accept was that I wasn't responsible for their deaths. It would have happened regardless of who was there with me or where my head was. Looking back, even though I was stressed over Mercy, I was on top of my fucking game out there. I'd been trained to be the best of the fucking best, and goddamn it, I was.

Two weeks ago, I called up Johnson's widow. I was alone

at Corps Security and I took a chance. I never fathomed that she would regret this hate-filled letter in my hands. She told me that she had wanted to contact me so many times over the years but just didn't know how. We talked for two hours that day. Remembering her husband, laughing about the stupid shit we would get into overseas, and finally healing. When I hung up the phone with her and felt that guilt dissipate a little, I started to believe in that hope for a blessed life.

My next call was to Morris's widow. She was shocked to hear from me but, in the end, glad that I called. Like Mary, she needed that closure that her husband hadn't suffered and to have some memories I could give her of him.

By the time I finished those calls, I broke.

I sat in my office, surrounded by computers and technical equipment, and I fought with my body to calm down. It was almost as if I hadn't known how to move on without that guilt. But by the time I left the office, I almost felt whole.

After removing Mary's letter—and my Medal of Honor—I walk into the kitchen. Then I swipe one of the lighters out of the spare drawer, place my medal on the counter, and hold her letter over the sink. With one flick of my thumb, I watch as flames take over the old paper. Each piece of ash that falls into the sink represents the guilt I'm letting go.

When I'm finished, I grab the medal and walk over to the mantel. I stand there with my legs planted to the ground, my shoulders tight, and take in the pictures Emmy insisted on putting up. Just one of the many home-decorating projects she forced me to do for her during her recovery.

There are five frames in all. The first is a picture of our group of friends from Axel and Izzy's wedding with Emmy and me standing on opposite ends of the crowd. I am looking—unsmiling—at the camera and she's looking directly at me. Even though it could hurt to look at this picture, I have to remind myself of what it represents—just how far we've come since.

The second is one we had taken when Greg and Melissa had everyone over for a late welcome home for the twins. Melissa hadn't wanted to do it without Emmy. Emmy is sitting off to the side, one of their girls resting against her good arm and her leg propped up on the couch. She was in so much pain that day but refused to let it stand in the way of going. You would never be able to tell by the look on her face. She's smiling down at Lillian—or Lila, as we've been instructed by her big brother, Cohen, to call her—with a look of pure wonderment. I made a mental promise to myself that day that I would put that look back in her eyes—only, this time, with our own children.

I run my finger over her profile in that picture and move on to the next.

It's one of all of the guys. Axel has his arm wrapped around Greg's neck—laughing. Beck is standing with Coop, their heads thrown back hooting, and I'm looking at them all pissed as hell. I let out a laugh when I remember why. Izzy can be seen in the background with Sway, both of them bent at their waists to hold their laughing bodies up. It took me three days until I stopped finding gold flecks of glitter on my skin. Another week until my head stopped shining in places.

"Damn Sway and his fucking glitter," I mumble with a smile.

The next is one we had taken when Chelcie came home from the hospital with Zac. All of us met down at Coop's grave and had

Davey take a picture. Everyone was there. Emmy, still unable to walk, was in my arms. Even though this picture breaks my heart because of the reminder that we no longer have Coop with us, to look from the first one when Emmy and I were so far from this moment and then to see us together… Yeah, it is hands down one of my favorite pictures. It's our whole family. All four of the men I consider brothers with the women they love. My girl is in my arms, her smile taking over her face and my small grin stealing the hardness from my face. Izzy is holding Nate while Axel is holding her very pregnant stomach. Greg and Melissa each hold one of their beautiful daughters. Beck has his arms wrapped around Dee. Asher and Chelcie are sitting on the ground next to Coop's headstone with sad smiles on their faces. In their arms is Coop's son, Zac. And then there are Sway and Cohen—both with red capes flowing in the wind, hands on their hips, and smiles on their lips. Sway said that we needed to make this a place where we could smile at and not always cry…so that's what he did.

The last picture I take in, the one that sits in the largest frame front and center, is the one of just Emmy and me. I didn't even know it had been taken, but I could kiss whoever did. We're both asleep in my bed—something we did a lot over her recovery. So often that the women in our circle took it upon themselves to come by—often—and make sure there wasn't anything needed. They would let themselves in and out, sometimes not even telling us they were here. I knew they were coming; my security system would trip them up every time.

In the picture, I have my back propped up against the headboard and Emmy is lying between my legs with her head on my thigh. She had fallen asleep rubbing the skin above my stump in a soft caress. I remember feeling her lips press against my knee right before her body went slack and her hand fell to rest where my leg stopped. That was the first and only time I ever let anyone freely touch my leg like that. She didn't judge or flinch; she accepted it and loved me even more because of my scars. Then I fell asleep with my head tipped back and a smile on my face that didn't even leave in my slumber.

I straighten out each frame before taking my Medal of Honor—one I never felt worthy of—and placing it right next to that picture of Emmy and me. Right next to the woman who made me believe that I was worthy of everything blessed in my life.

With a nod, I walk back to the bedroom and climb into the bed to pull Emmy into my arms.

Right where she belongs.

# CHAPTER 31
## Emmy

I IMMEDIATELY NOTICE his medal on the mantel the next morning. Maddox was fast asleep when I woke up. It took me a while to get into the living room, but when I did, it was the first thing I saw. I don't make a big production over it; I smile and continue my slow hobble into the kitchen to get some water.

It is when I stand over the sink, empty glass ready and hand hovering over the cold-water knob, that I see the ashes. The meaning of such a monumental move on his end hits me like a train. Straight through my chest and slamming into my heart.

He finds me on the floor in the kitchen. I'm naked as the day I was born with silent tears streaming down my face.

"Em? Jesus Christ, are you okay?" His hands roam over my body. Then he checks my newly freed arm and looks down to my leg to make sure there isn't an obvious source to my pain.

I just sit there and look into his handsome face, my breathing coming in fast pants. These damn tears won't stop. His thumbs work overtime trying to stop their falling while he cups my face between his palms.

"You did it," I sob.

He looks at me in question. His head tilts slightly to the side, his strong brows pulled tight. "I'm not following, angel. Are you hurt?"

"You let them go and you didn't need me," I gasp.

"Emersyn, fucking hell—what is wrong?!" His voice booms through the room and I smile. The tears don't stop, but I smile huge and look into his eyes. "Have you lost your mind? Do you need me to find some happy pills? For the love of Christ, Em, what is wrong?"

He's losing his patience and I'm losing my damn mind.

I reach up, lightly rub my palm against his chest, right above his heart, and look at him with what I hope is the face of a crazy woman who loves him. The tears aren't going to stop. I've been waiting and hoping that he would let go of just one of those three demons in his box. I knew they were the biggest of his burdens, and even though I was willing to carry them with him for an eternity, I wanted him to feel peace.

"I love you, my big, strong, and brave man."

He is clearly having trouble following my mood swings because he seems even more confused than before. I work harder to control my crazy, stifling my tears and swallowing the heavy lump in my throat.

"I knew you would be able to do it, baby. I can't even tell you how proud I am of you right now."

To my utter and complete shock, his cheeks heat and Maddox Locke freaking blushes. "It was time, Em," is all he says.

"Yeah, I guess it was," I agree.

"Come on. Let's get you back to bed."

When we get in the bedroom, I toss one glance at the box still sitting on his dresser. I know that, by it still being there, there is still one more thing left. I'm guessing that, since his Medal is out and the letter from his fallen brother's widow was the one to go, that means the hardest and largest of his demons is left.

Those bastards in Texas.

As we slowly walk towards the bed, I can't help but feel a little nervous over the enormity of which battle is left for him. It won't be easy, but I won't let him do it alone.

He helps me climb into bed, and when he moves to leave, I look up at him and shake my head.

"Sit," I command.

His lips twitch and his brow cocks, but he sits.

"Tell me how to remove your prosthetic please?"

His eyes go wide, showing me his shock. "Em," he starts.

"Don't make me spank your ass, Maddox Locke. Tell me how to remove it."

He grumbles under his breath, but he takes my hand and moves me through the motions. It's hard since one of my hands is throbbing from having not been used for so long. I'm twisted at a weird angle in the bed, but I manage to remove it. Then he takes it from my hands and places it next to the bed. He won't meet my eye, and I hate that he still feels some shame.

"Come on. Scoot back," I demand, patting the bed next to me.

He gripes and complains but still sits by me.

I reach down and place my hand against his hip. He jumps slightly but still doesn't meet my eyes. It isn't until my hand has moved to rest right above his stump that his head snaps to the side and his eyes take mine.

"The next time I see even an ounce of shame darkening those sexy, black eyes of yours, Maddox, I'm going to smack your ass until it's pink."

His jaw drops, but I keep going.

"And then, if you still act like this part of you that I love is something you should hate, I'll punish you every time. You think that I don't love every inch of this magnificent body? Oh, you are so wrong. This part of you that you feel shame in is something I look at with pride. You, my brave, brave man, are a hero and it's time you started wearing that title with pride. Be as proud of yourself as I am. Maybe I should just start keeping myself from you until you see just how much I mean this."

I go to move my hand to my sex and his eyes flash for a second before his strong hand grips my wrist—softly but with enough pressure to show me that he means business.

"If you think you're going to keep that sweet goddamn cunt from me, then you've got another thing coming, Emersyn." His voice rushes through me, and I have to shift my hips when my arousal becomes too much. "You don't keep your body from me… ever. Understand?"

"I'll do what I have to do," I sass back.

"Emersyn," he growls.

"I don't think so, mister! You aren't going to go all sexy, growling alpha on me. You heard what I said. Now calm your cock down and take the over-the-top caveman down a peg or two. You still think of your imperfections as something to be ashamed of?"

He scowls, but answers, "No, Emmy, I don't. But that doesn't mean I have to fucking like them."

"That's where you're wrong, big boy." With a smile, I run my hand over his hardened skin. He shivers, but I know he isn't cold. "You'll fucking like them, because *your woman* fucking loves them."

"I should wash your mouth out with soap and then spank your ass."

"I would enjoy that too much."

He groans and drops his head back with a loud thump against the headboard. "I don't hate it, okay? You are the only person who has ever even touched me like this besides someone medically responsible to. I'm working on the rest. I don't hide it from you and you have to know that, months ago, I would still be keeping it covered whenever I knew your eyes could take sight of it."

"I get that. But it's time to stop playing in the dark, baby."

"Meaning?" he barks.

"Ugh, you are so frustrating. Meaning that, tomorrow, when we go to family dinner, I want you in shorts."

His eyes go from hard to shocked within seconds. "It's fucking winter!" he snarls.

"I don't give a crap if you're headed to the North Pole. Shorts, Maddox. It's time to toss that ridiculous fear that others will judge you out the damn window."

"That damn sass," he drones.

"You love *that damn sass*," I retort.

"You're damn fucking right I do."

Then he shows me just how much he loves *that damn sass*. It isn't until hours later, when our bodies are still covered with a light layer of sweat, that I allow myself one huge mental victory dance.

# CHAPTER 32
## Emmy

GREG AND Melissa's house is full-out chaos when we arrive. Babies are crying everywhere. Cohen and Sway are running around the lower level of their house with underwear on their heads and capes flapping behind them. Dee is lying on the loveseat because she hasn't stopped throwing up for, what she calls 'an eternity.' Izzy rolls her eyes from the chair where she's nursing Danielle, their month-old baby.

"Don't you roll your eyes at me, Izzy Reid! Just give me a second to get up and I'm going to kick your ass." Dee tries to stand but then holds her hand over her mouth with wide eyes.

"I'm guessing this means she's about to blow chunks all over the place?" I laugh.

Her eyes water with the effort it takes her to push aside her sickness. And then she locks her hormonal-driven fury on me. "Emmy! Don't even start with me. I can't wait for you to be throwing up every two seconds!"

Maddox goes solid next to me as he helps me walk into the house. I look up and try to figure out what he's thinking, but his face is completely void of emotion. Whatever. I'll pick it out of him later.

"Don't tell her that," Chelcie scolds, walking into the room with Zac sleeping against her chest. "It isn't that bad. Plus, it's worth it." She smiles at Zac and sits down next to Dee.

The movement is obviously not what her stomach needed because she jumps up and runs to the bathroom.

Once we stop laughing, I move to my side and drop down onto the couch. I wait for Maddox to sit next to me, but when I look over, he's still standing where I left him. His eyes are darting around the room with worry.

"Why don't you head out to the backyard, Mad?" Melissa asks from the doorway. "The guys doing that macho thing you all do when you stand around a grill and grunt." She laughs and gives him a quick hug.

He looks around the room for a second before making his way past the girls and outside. I keep my eyes on them and wait to see when they notice. None of them watch as he walks by even though his shorts give him no way to hide the one thing he feels shame over. Well, this certainly is going better than I thought. I know he was worried there would be some big gasp and fanfare, but he should have known our friends a little better than that.

"Hey!" a small voice screams from the kitchen. "Look, Dilbert! Maddox Locke is a transformer! MOMMY! I wanna be a transformer just like Maddox Locke!" Cohen comes rushing into the room, crashing into the wall when his socks don't let him stop. Then he jumps off the floor with a big, toothy grin. "Mommy, did you see?! It's soooo cool!"

I don't breathe, afraid of how this is going to play out. I want to rush to Maddox and make sure that he's okay, but I know that wouldn't help. He needs to learn to get past this one all on his own.

"Yeah, Co, I saw," she laughs. "You can't be a transformer though." His little face falls and she rushes on. "Baby boy, you can't just decide to be a transformer. Only special people get that honor and only God can pick them. But you know what? That means that Maddox is an even bigger superhero. He's is a transformer because he saved people."

My eyes prickle and I listen as Melissa gives a child version of why my big, strong man is a hero.

As they continue to talk about how 'cool' Maddox is, I use that time to look at the faces of the others in the room. Dee still looks a little green, but like the others, she has a small smile on her face.

One thing lacking on all of their faces, though, is shock.

When Cohen leaves the room, I direct my question to the room at large. "How long have you guys known?"

"Uh, maybe about a month after I met him," Izzy starts. "His jeans had gotten stuck and were folded in the back."

"Took about six months for me. He was sitting and had his leg crossed over… I guess it pushed the hem up. I don't know," Melissa states indifferently.

"He fell—well, to be honest, I knocked his ass over—one day and saw it. He knows that I know," Dee states, trying to keep her sickness from taking over. I watch her suck in a few deep breaths before she looks back at me with a shrug.

"I can't remember when I found out. I figured he didn't want to talk about it since it wasn't common knowledge," Chelcie says with a smile.

"I can't believe you guys never told me," I fuss.

"Seriously, Em. I think we all just figured, when he was ready, we would know. Or whatever," Dee says.

"Well you could have made my job a little easier!" I snap.

"What changed his mind?" Izzy asks with a frown.

"He was ready. He just needed a little push." I cross my arms and smile brightly at my closest friends. "Now bring me a baby," I demand.

Two seconds later, little Lyndsie is in my arms and I sigh with contentment.

DINNER WENT off without a hitch. I knew it would, even if I was a little worried about what would happen if we had some sort of weird reaction. Cohen was the icebreaker we needed, and by the time we get home, Maddox's mood is even lighter.

He's just one more baby step closer to being free of the things that haunt him. I know he might not like the talk I have planned for tonight, but it's time, and after seeing him take this last step tonight, I know he's ready.

"HEY."

He looks over at me from the other side of the couch with a grin.

"Can we talk about something?"

He mutes the television and turns his attention back to me. "What's up, Em?" He takes a deep breath, and I know he's thinking the worst.

"Come here first," I request, patting the cushion next to me.

He places his iPad down on the coffee table and moves over. Then, much to my surprise, he lifts me off the couch and places my ass in his lap. I loop my arms around his neck and give him a soft kiss. His body visibly relaxes some at that.

"Calm down, baby," I whisper against his cheek before giving him another kiss.

"I think it's safe to say that I'm not going to like whatever we're going to talk about, so forgive me if I can't just calm down, Em."

"Right. Well, maybe I'll surprise you?"

He just chuckles and pulls me closer.

"I want to go to Texas." There. I said it. It's out there. Now, he can just accept it.

*Yeah, right.* Ugh, I shouldn't have blurted that out.

"You what?" he thunders.

"Okay—I'll admit that I should have led up to that."

"You fucking think?"

"Hey! I don't know what you're getting pissed about, Maddox. I haven't even explained myself." I go to bring my arms down from around his neck, but he quickly moves to hold them in place.

His face moves close and his nose touches mine. "Why in the hell do you want to go to Texas, Em?"

"Because it's time," I state calmly. I hold his gaze, and after what feels like the longest time, he drops his forehead to mine.

"I don't want you near them, Em. I don't want you close

enough for them to get their claws into you."

There. Now he's said it—the one thing I know was still holding him back.

He's afraid that, if I get near his family—that 'temptation of power,' he calls it—and their evil, it might suck me in.

My heart breaks for him.

"Talk to me. Please. Tell me what's going through your head."

He doesn't speak, his forehead still against mine.

"Maddox, baby?" I press.

"I'm terrified, Emmy. I am downright terrified that they could hurt you."

"I'm a lot tougher than you're giving me credit for here, Maddox."

"I know you are, but they're… Jesus. I don't even know how to explain it." He pulls back and looks into my eyes. "This is important to you?"

"Very." I don't say anything else. I let his eyes study my own and wait.

"You want that box in hell, yeah?"

I nod my head.

"All right. Let's get you fixed up and then we'll head to Texas. I don't think I need to go this far to let that go, but I'm willing to give it a try. But, Em? The second—and I mean the very second—that I think that you're in danger, we are fucking gone."

I smile huge. My-face-hurts huge. He just shakes his head and gives me a deep kiss.

# CHAPTER 33
## Maddox

### FOUR MONTHS LATER

I WALK HAND in hand with Emmy through the Dallas/Fort Worth International Airport. Her smile keeps me from falling apart. I'm a mix of dread, trepidation, and anger. Just being back in this state has my skin crawling. It's like every year that I've been gone, pushed myself to forget, is just gone in a giant wash.

I've come so far, and I think that, deep down, I'm worried more that this trip will be one giant setback.

"Stop."

I look down at her, my angel—and the reason I'm even able to be here right now—and scowl.

"Stop what, woman?"

"Stop worrying. I got your back." She lifts one tiny fist up and waits for me to give her a bump.

I roll my eyes, but give her what she wants.

"Plus, if things get tough, you can always transform and go all Autobot on their asses." She lets out a loud laugh and I just shake my head.

Ever since the night she demanded I wear shorts, I haven't hidden myself from anyone. I expected to feel their pity or maybe for them to stare, but no one acted any differently. I get questions from Cohen, but that's it. The guys don't bring it up, but they know how big that moment was.

This is the last speed bump that stands in my way—in our way—of the future we deserve. Especially now that her parents and that motherfucker, Shawn, are taken care of.

Shawn, may he rot in fucking hell, didn't last a month in jail. He made enemies quickly, and one beautiful morning, his body was found in his cell.

I took Emmy out to dinner that night to celebrate. Well, she didn't know that was why, but I did. It felt fucking good to know that, while I was taking my girl to dinner, her laughter and smiles warming my heart, the bastard who'd tried to take her from me was rotting six feet deep.

Her parents took a little more time. She doesn't talk about them and I know it's all part of her one-step-forward-without-looking-back approach, but not me. Hell fucking no. I wasn't going to sit back and let them continue to live some twisted life. They needed to pay for what they had done to her. So she might not have talked—but I did.

It took four months after we left for all of my planning to come to fruition. That club had to go first. It really was a shame that a homeless man happened to throw his cigarette next to the building when a pile of gasoline-soaked rags had been carelessly thrown there.

With Syn gone, it was only a matter of time.

I didn't think they would last that long without their moneymaker, but it was two weeks before I was able to get them for prostitution of minors. I can rest easy knowing that there isn't a chance in hell they'll touch my girl now.

When I asked her the other night if she wanted to talk about them, she simply said no. She only wanted to know one thing—if they could get to her again. I gave her one hell of a kiss and reassured her that they would never be able to touch any part of her life again. She doesn't want details, but I know she feels the relief of knowing that.

With her family taken care of, all that is left is mine. I just hope that I can feel the same satisfaction as I do now when we fly out of here tomorrow night.

The drive to the hotel doesn't take long. My family's estate is about thirty minutes away. I'm close enough that it won't take long to get there but far enough away that I can't feel their vile vortex sucking me in. Fuck, my skin is still crawling.

I drop our shared suitcase on the floor and turn to where she's putting her purse down and checking her phone. She's been texting Melissa since we landed to keep her updated. She asked me if she could tell her what wouldn't break my trust but enough that she could have someone to be there to confide in. I don't want her to feel like she has to keep this all in and on herself. The guys all know, so even though I didn't want Melissa to know just how fucked up my life was, I agreed that she needed someone to talk to about it all. Especially knowing that this weekend is most likely going to be one big fuck-up.

I hear her toss her phone on the table and look up to see her full lips smirking at me. Her hands fisted at her hips and pure mischief is in her eyes.

"So…how about you stop standing there worrying like an old lady and come fuck your woman."

God, I love this girl.

"You getting sassy with me, Emersyn?" I question while stalking over to where she's standing.

She doesn't flinch. Instead, she stands up straighter and raises her eyebrows.

"Oh, I'm sassing you all right. Planning on doing something about it? Or maybe I need to just go take a nice, long bath and take care of myself?"

"Like fucking hell," I grumble. Then I bend, grasp her hips, and toss her onto the bed.

She laughs before snapping her mouth shut when she sees my eyes.

"You want me to fuck you?"

She nods, licking her lips.

"You want me to pink your sweet ass?"

Her eyes go bright with lust and she nods again.

"And what if I refuse?"

"You wouldn't," she gasps, rolling and coming up on her knees. "Well, then, I will go take a nice. Long. Shower!"

"Oh I damn well would if you think you can still threaten to take your pussy from me."

"Oh come on, Mad! I was just joking!"

I slowly pull my belt from my jeans. Her eyes shoot down and widen. My lips turn up when I see the desire—the craving—taking hold of her. Walking over to the edge of the bed, I bend the belt and slap it against my palm. She jumps at the sound and gulps.

"You need to stop threatening to take that sweet pussy from

me, Em. I don't like thinking about not having your sweet juices coating my cock or running down my chin when I eat you. I don't like the thought of my fingers not fucking you hard while you beg for my cock. So let me ask you again… If I refuse?"

She whimpers.

"Emersyn. If I refuse to fuck you?"

She gulps audibly again and lets out a shaky breath. "Then I guess I'm going to have to wait until you're ready, *master*, to fuck me."

"Don't get snippy, Emersyn. It doesn't suit you. And remember this: I'm not your fucking master. I don't want to control you. Everything I do to your body is so that you feel pleasure. I don't spank your ass for any other reason but to make your fucking body electric with want. When my hand comes down and your cunt weeps with your cream all because what I'm doing to you turns you on that much—baby, you have no idea what that does to me. I want to share your pleasure, and the thought of you taking one second of that from me so that you can come at your own hand… Well, that's just not fucking acceptable."

"Maddox, please shut up and either eat me or fuck me. I don't care, but please just take me."

Her nipples are poking through her thin blouse. Her eyes are hooded and her chest is moving fast—her full tits calling for my mouth.

"Get naked."

She doesn't pause at my command. Her shirt and bra are all but ripped off before she scrambles to her feet and stands before me. She gives me a heated glance before shoving her jeans and panties down. Then she stands tall and waits.

She waits for *me* to tell her what to do next, and damn if that isn't the hottest thing.

I drop the belt and almost laugh when she sighs. My girl wanted to feel that leather against her skin. I'll give it to her, but it won't be in some hotel room. No, I'll give that to her when she can scream the walls down.

My shirt comes off next before I watch her talk herself into reaching out. Then my hands fall to my jeans. A flip of my wrist and they fall. She swallows thickly when my cock jumps free, the head already wet with pre-come.

"You want my cock in your mouth first? Or do you want me to eat you? Because, baby, right now, that's up to you."

"Can I have both?" she asks devilishly.

"Fuck me," I laugh. "Yeah, baby, you damn sure can."

I sit and finish pulling my jeans off. She drops to her knees so quickly I can't stop her, giving me a long lick up my shaft before going about removing my leg. I don't speak. I just watch her. When she finishes, I lean back.

"Get that pussy up here and let me feast, woman."

She giggles as she climbs onto the bed. When she kneels just above my head, I look up at her wet pussy. Spreading her legs, she scoots forward slowly. Fuck this.

I grab her hips and pull her roughly to my mouth. She falls towards the bed before catching herself. I feel her hot breaths dancing across my tight skin and groan against her core. She doesn't waste a second before wrapping one slim hand around my cock and pumping softly. When I feel her tongue come out and lick around my swollen head, I bite her clit.

After that, she moans around my cock as we feast on each other. Her tongue is swirling around each one of the bars on my shaft and circling around my girth. When she pulls on the ring pierced through the head, I grunt.

Then I bring my hand down hard on her ass. She pulls off my cock and screams. *Yeah, that's right, Em. Fucking swallow that cock.*

I know she's getting close, and as much as I want to feel her wetness on my face, right now, I want her coming on my cock.

She gets one long swipe of my tongue before I pull back and kiss her quivering thigh. I can feel my dick pressed against the back of her throat, and I wait for her to move her head up before I slap her ass again.

"Get up here and ride my cock, Emersyn."

She fumbles and almost falls headfirst off the bed, but after she gets herself steady she turns and climbs up my body. Her lips hit mine and her tongue comes out to lick herself from my lips and tongue. Then she impales herself, causing us both to cry out.

"Fucking hell, Em. Best fucking pussy ever. That's right, angel. Ride that cock hard." I smack her ass twice.

Her lips crash back to mine as she takes my body just as hard as I knew she would. My hips thrust to meet hers and my hands stay on her waist to help drive her down on my hard flesh. My balls—so painfully tight—slap against her with each slam.

Her nails are pressed deep into the skin on my shoulders. The moans that are rolling off her tongue are like some sort of delicious song. A song that drugs my senses and has me yelling out my release just seconds after her walls clamp down and her juices—that delicious fucking honey—coats my balls.

When she breaks the silence with, “I think we need to work on that roaring, you sexy man,” a smile breaks out on my face and I throw my head back and laugh.

# CHAPTER 34
## *Emmy*

THIS IS it.

This is the moment I've been waiting for him to be ready for.

But as we stand in front of the massive house that radiates the malevolence that is his family, I feel fear stark, cold terror.

I have no doubt that he's ready to tackle this. My faith in him isn't in question. No, my terror is all my own. I have felt nothing but raw hate since he told me of his horrifying past. Each pain that these people inflicted on him fills me with the kind of anger I never thought I was capable of feeling.

I want to physically harm them. I crave a weapon that would put their blood on my hands. Even when I was stuck back at Syn and living my own personal hell, I never felt this kind of energy literally take over my being.

Every second we stand here only makes it worse, until I'm positive that I could lash out with just a flip of my hand and shoot lightning from my hands.

This isn't about me or my inner rage over how he was treated. This moment is all for him, and I will do everything in my power to remain a silent strength by his side.

My eyes roam the home in front of us. Each brick, I hate. The large floor-to-ceiling windows that line the first floor of the home make my fingers twitch for a rock—or maybe a flaming bag of horseshit tied to a rock followed by a grenade. The wraparound drive is lined with flowers and bushes and shit that makes me want to jump back in our rental and start doing donuts in the grass. I had to talk myself out of grabbing the keys from Maddox when we got out of the car and I saw the shining, red sports car sitting in the drive. It would look wonderful with deeply gouged key slashes.

*Jesus, what is wrong with me?*

I look over at Maddox, expecting to see some dark essence in him over being back, but I just see a thoughtful expression. His jaw is relaxed, his eyes are searching, and not a single pained wrinkle is visible. I squeeze his hand and his eyes meet mine.

"You doing okay, big boy?"

"Yeah, angel. Shockingly, I'm okay. Ready to get this over with and get you back to the hotel."

"You would be thinking about *that* right now," I laugh, my mood feeling slightly less violent.

"That's keeping me from going off the hinges right now, so I'm going to go with what works."

I can give him that. If that's what he needs, then so be it.

"I think, maybe, we should knock or something. Unless they're evil little witches that somehow can sense our arrival."

"I wouldn't put it past them, Em. I really wouldn't."

Right, then. I reach out when it becomes clear he isn't going to knock and bang my fist against the enormous wooden door, using it to take some of my madness out. I pound until my fist tingles, not even stopping when I hear Maddox's deep chuckles.

"Pretty sure there isn't a question that we have arrived, baby."

"I could start kicking too. Don't you test me, Maddox."

"Wouldn't dream of it." He smiles and my heart skips a beat. Then he leans in until his lips hover next to my ear. "Watch that sass. You're turning me on."

My fist stops its banging and my jaw drops at his words. I'm seconds from turning towards him when the lock disengages and the door swings open.

"What the hell do you want?" The voice matches what I anticipated. Snarky.

Maddox doesn't react to coming face to face with his mother after almost twelve years. He just tilts his head to the side and gives her a little half smile.

Her eyes go from my fierce scowl to the man standing tall and proud next to me, and I watch with satisfaction as her eyes flash.

Fear.

Or maybe it's indigestion, but it looks a hell of a lot like fear.

"If it isn't my unruly little shit," she sneers.

"Invite us in, Diana." His voice holds no room for argument. Just looking at him, if I didn't know the kindness that lives within him, I would piss myself.

Of course, this bitch wouldn't notice a predator after its prey.

"I think you can just say whatever the hell you need to right here, Maddox. There is no need for you to dirty up my home with your filth."

"Bitch," I mumble under my breath.

She turns her head and looks over me from head to toe. I picked my outfit with care. I wanted to give her something to focus on if things went south. I can handle anything she throws at me, and if Maddox looks like he can't handle this at any second, then I'm prepared to work everything I have to gain her attention.

"Did you pick this one off the street?" Her eyes zero in on my short—very short—black shorts. They move to my tight—very tight—blood-red V-neck shirt. I lose points with the shoes though. I didn't want to risk anything going wrong by wearing the heels Dee had packed for me.

"You focus on me and not her. You hear me?" For the first time, his calm demeanor slips and his rage comes through.

"Mother?"

I feel Maddox jolt when the masculine voice comes from down the hall.

"Oh, for Christ's sake. I really don't have time for this." She turns and walks away from the door, leaving it wide open behind her.

I look over at Maddox and wait for him to make the next move. He takes a few deep breaths before walking over the threshold.

Right into hell.

"What the fuck is he doing here?"

I move from where I was trailing behind him and lock eyes with who I assume is his brother, Mason. Crap, he really got unlucky in the looks department. I think that, if I squint and maybe tilt my head to the side, I can see how he might have been attractive one day.

Now though? Now he looks like a middle-aged, fat-ass pervert I would have seen regularly at Syn. His thinning, light-brown hair is combed over, doing a terrible job at hiding the fact that he only has a few strands left until his shining scalp is naked. His beady eyes are bloodshot and his protruding gut is seriously testing the buttons on his *pink* dress shirt.

"Apparently, he has something to say, Mason. This should be interesting. To the study, Maddox. I trust you can find the way. I need a drink." She walks away and leaves the two brothers standing in the entryway.

If things come to blows, there is no question that Maddox will win. He towers over his brother. His thickly muscled body is a machine of power and his brother looks like he wouldn't even be able to open a pickle jar.

"Never thought I would see the day that the rat came crawling home." He laughs when Maddox snarls, shakes his head, and turns to walk away.

This time, Maddox doesn't need a second to consider if he will take the next steps. He stomps through the house, his boots sounding off the walls with thumping echoes. I double my stride to keep up with him, never once letting go of his hand.

After we have been standing in the study by ourselves for ten minutes, they enter. Only this time, there is a third person with them. Her blond hair hangs down her back in soft waves. Her blue eyes are hard and calculating. And much like his mom, Maddox's ex-fiancée is perfectly put together. My palms itch to tear her apart.

"Oh, this is fresh. I thought he was a cripple now?" she asks his brother while looking down at his legs.

I instantly notice the size of her wedding band—hell, it's hard to miss. How can she even keep her arm from dragging on the ground with that gaudy thing? And how could she have ever left Maddox for the weasel next to her?

"It's called an amputee, Mercedes."

Her eyes snap to his. "That's the same thing, bastard."

Maddox laughs and I look over at him with a smile, my heart light when I realize that I worried for nothing. He's too strong to let them hurt him.

"Sit the fuck down," he thunders.

Their eyes widen slightly, but they don't recognize the threat in front of them.

"Get it over with," Mason grumbles.

"Don't worry, *big brother,*" he sneers. "I won't take up too much of your precious fucking time. I just have a few things to say and then we will leave."

I'm guessing that the arrival of her long-lost lover was too shocking for her to notice the other woman in the room. I recognize a threatened woman when I see one. After all, I've been watching her husband rake his eyes over me with lust-filled want for the last ten minutes. This is one crazy madwoman.

"Who the fuck is she?" Her question isn't directed at me, but I answer anyway.

"Emersyn. It's a pleasure. And, sweet cheeks, I'm his future wife."

I don't know what made me say it. Maybe I just wanted to slap it in her face that I won the priced Locke. Or maybe it was just wishful yapping. Either way, the words taste delicious.

The hand Maddox has wrapped around mine flexes, but he doesn't outwardly react—nor does he dispute my words.

"HA! You mean you actually found someone who you think loves you? That's hilarious."

I take a page from Maddox's book and growl deep in my throat.

"Shut the fuck up, Mercedes." Maddox scolds.

She huffs at his reprimand, but she does shut her mouth.

"I was thinking one night that I never knew why you hated me so much. It just didn't make sense to me that you could give birth to someone and hate them instantly with everything you had. I really don't give a fuck what your reasons are now, but let me tell *you* a little fucking bedtime story this time. There once was a man who thought he was broken and unworthy. A demon that walked the Earth, causing nothing but pain to others with only a touch. Then he met an angel that was just as lost as he was, and he realized, with her help, that it was never *him* that was broken. It was never *him* that spread his villainous evil. You see, that evil that he was told he had been born with… It came from only one person—*you*. And once that man was free from the webs of her darkness, he realized he wasn't some giant fuck-up. He had just been born from evil and it took a little longer to clean that bullshit from his skin."

"Now you little—"

"You don't fucking get to speak!" he bellows. "Let me ask you, Diana. How many years have you been afraid that I would show back up? That I would question everything you told me when I was at my worst? I should have thought about it sooner, but I've been a little busy since. It didn't take long for me to sit at my computer and tap into your lives with just a few keystrokes. You made a mistake though. When you went to sell the company, I'm assuming because you were either drunk or had spent all of your worth, you couldn't do anything without the one person who still holds twenty-five percent of Locke Oil, could you?"

I want to snap my eyes to his. The shock of what he's saying is making my head spin. I didn't even know about this.

"Ah, I can tell by your shocked and wonderfully terrified faces that you really did think I would never find out. Isn't it just fucking good fortune that I showed up when I did? I don't fucking want your company. I didn't when you assumed I did and I didn't when I was fighting to rebuild my life twelve years ago. But you can be sure of one fucking thing—I don't care if it sinks you in the ground. You want my shares—take them. I know you need my signature to sell and you need to sell just to keep afloat."

I can see the wheels turning in their heads. They think they've won.

"Just like that?" Mason asks.

"Just fucking like that. Oh…I forgot. I won't accept a check since I'm pretty sure it would bounce to the fucking moon. You want them, then be prepared to bleed that money you don't fucking have."

"We don't have that kind of money," his brother fumes.

"Well, then, I guess I'm not fucking going anywhere." He laughs.

"Is this what you think will intimidate us? Coming into *my* home with your slut and acting like we give a shit?"

My eyes narrow at Mercedes.

"That's the thing, Mercedes. I don't really give a shit what you think."

"You loved me once." It sounds like she is trying to talk herself into that one.

"I didn't fucking love you. I'll admit I thought I did, but that's what happens when you have a bitch willing to spread her legs. You were easy, Mercedes. Let's not get that thought crossed with any affection you might think I have left for you."

"You were going to marry me."

"Jesus fuck, Mercy! I'm right fucking here," his brother yelps.

"Diana," Maddox speaks, ignoring the domestic argument happening between his brother and sister-in-law. "Find your precious lawyer, Jefferson, and get this shit rolling. I don't really give a damn if you have to sell this very house to be able to afford to buy me out. You want it that much, make it happen."

She doesn't look happy about it, but she stomps out of the room.

Before she can get too far, Maddox calls out for her. I watch has she walks back in with a little less supremacy than she had earlier.

"And you, Mason. You might think you've won. You have the girl you think I want. You have this shithole in Texas and a company six months from bankruptcy. But, *brother,* you will never have the world because I already fucking found it. I'm worth more than you will ever see in your lifetime and I'm not only talking about the money piling up in my bank. I have everything you wish you had. And the best thing? I have a woman who loves me for everything I am and ever will be. One who isn't just with me because of some purse or shoe she wants at the moment. So… Check. Mate. Motherfucker."

"I'll fucking kill you," he spits.

"You could fucking try, but even with my hands tied behind my back, I would snap you in two."

Mason's face goes pale before he storms out of the room, slamming the door in his wake. His mother hasn't moved from her spot. She looks at Maddox with shock and maybe a little respect.

"Maybe I underestimated you, stupid boy. I'll have Jefferson send you the paperwork." She shakes her head and follows his brother out of the room.

"Looks like it's just us, Mercedes. I do have a question for you. Why?"

She crosses her bone-thin arms over her chest and huffs. "That, Maddox, is easy. Mason promised me the fucking world. The best clothes, houses, cars. Ultimate power right at my fingertips. All I had to do was get you out of the picture somehow. It seemed so simple at first. You had given me the perfect plan when you put that speck of glass on my hand. I just had to play my cards right and fake a few orgasms. That meeting before you shipped out was all my idea. We just had to throw a few lines of bullshit out there and wait for your temper to get the best of you. I knew you wouldn't question what they were saying. Not only are you just too fucking stupid, but when I dropped the baby bomb on you, all of your focus went into worrying about that." She laughs and my rage grows. "You didn't even question the baby. You just believed me because you *loved* me. God, you were so fucking stupid."

"What do you fucking mean, I believed you? I saw the picture of you, Mason, and the baby."

Her laughter takes on an insane crackle. Just the volume of it screams psycho. "Ah, yes. Perfect timing struck again when we decided to go visit a friend of your brother's who had had their first little baby. Some careful editing and you couldn't tell a difference. I knew you would buy it at face value. There never was a baby." She laughs again, and that rage that was building hits a boiling point.

"You see," she says while stepping forward and dragging her fingertip down his chest. "I just needed to make sure you were distracted, and digging that final nail into your heart was the perfect way. You wouldn't have come back—you had too much fucking pride for that. And since, unfortunately for me, my plan to have you so distracted that you got yourself blown the fuck up didn't work and all you lost was your stupid leg."

Oh, I did not just hear her say that.

"You. Fucking. Bitch!" I scream and drop Maddox hand. I hear him stress my name before I turn into a human torpedo and launch my body into hers.

She doesn't stand a chance against me. I have too much frenzied madness burning away at my veins. I land on her and latch on like a monkey until we both slam to the ground. I can hear Maddox yelling my name, but he doesn't attempt to pull me off.

"You motherfucking bitch!" I yell before punching her in the face. My fist hits her jaw first. Then I shift my weight when she tries to throw me off her and give her another hard slam into her ribs. "I'll kill you! I will!" I get three more slaps in before I'm being lifted off her. I look down and spit on her. "You never deserved him. I thank my lucky stars that you were too fucking STUPID to realize just what kind of man you had. Take a good look, bitch, because you will never know what it feels like to be with a REAL man!" I spit again and smile when it lands right between her eyes.

She moves to stand and Maddox isn't quick enough to get me away from her. I lift up my foot and kick her right in the ass, laughing when she falls forward and knocks into the bookshelf, sending a few dozen books from the shelves onto her prone form.

"You feel better?" Maddox asks with a huge smile on his handsome face.

"Yeah," I reply, smoothing out my hair and clothes. "I do.

How about you, baby?"

His eyes go soft and he gives me a kiss. "Yeah, angel. I've never felt better in my life."

Looking into his eyes, I believe it. Until I feel a sharp pain in my side and wetness against my panties.

*What the hell?*

I reach down, and when I bring my hands up, there is blood on my fingertips.

"Maddox?"

"Yeah, Em?" he asks, moving his eyes from where Mercedes still hasn't moved. When he meets mine, he goes still. "Em?"

"I think it might be a good idea if we go to a hospital," I whisper.

He looks from my eyes to my hand before his tan skin goes white and I'm in his arms. He doesn't respond when his mother snarls his name or when his brother starts stalking after him.

He doesn't stop until he's slamming the car in park and carrying me into the local emergency room doors.

# CHAPTER 35
## Maddox

SHE WAS right. Letting go of that last tie gave me a sense of peace I hadn't fathomed possible. I didn't feel pain from my mother's or brother's words. I didn't even flinch when Mercedes told me just how deep her deceit had been. I even wanted to laugh when Emmy threw her body on top of her and fought her like a world-class boxer.

I felt whole for the first time in my life. The weight of those monsters that had been eating away at me for so long—gone. I didn't think there was one thing I could feel wrong.

That is until I looked over at Emmy and saw fear in her eyes. At first, I didn't know what was happening. Then I saw the blood on her hands. My confusion turned into a fear as cold as ice filling my veins.

We were taken right back and she was immediately checked out. My world was rocked an hour later.

Emmy. Pregnant.

I look over at her as she rests peacefully in the hospital bed. They gave her intravenous fluids to help rehydrate her and an antibiotic. According to the doctor, she—and the baby—are fine for the moment. He couldn't see any sign of a miscarriage. After we briefly explained that she had been in a physical altercation, he said that it was most likely a threatened miscarriage and that she would need to stay off her feet then follow up with her doctor when we get home.

"Hey," she sighs, turning in the bed and curling on her side to look at me. "You okay?"

I can't help it. I throw my head back and laugh. The tension that was rolling off my body and all the stress of the day evaporates with just the sound of her voice.

"I should probably be concerned that you're losing it." Her lips are curled in a beautiful smile, and even though she looks tired, I can see that she's happy.

"You took years off my life earlier, Emmy."

"I'm sorry," she says honestly.

"You're okay?" I search her eyes for any signs that she might not be happy about this news.

"I'm perfect."

As simple as that.

Perfect.

"This is a blessing, Maddox," she sighs, her gorgeous, honey eyes hopeful that I'll see it that way.

Blessing.

There's that word again. One that I never thought I could attach to my life. But now, looking at her curled in front of me—carrying our child—our love wrapped around us like a tight embrace… Yeah, it damn sure is a blessing.

"That it is, angel. That. It. Is." I lean over and kiss her softly before I grab her hand, and try to figure out how to tell her how much this means to me. "I love you." It really is just as simple as that. Her love started it all, and she never gave up until I believed her. "You made me whole again, Emmy. You drove those monsters and nightmares from my soul and replaced them with something so unbelievable that I'm not even sure if I understand the enormity of its power. I'll never stop fighting to make sure that I continue to be worthy of that love, baby."

"I love you back, my big, strong man."

"One thing, Em?" I wait until her eyes come back to mine. "Future wife, huh?" I laugh lightly when she blushes one hell of a hot shade of pink.

When she said that earlier, the only thing I could think of was how fast I could drag her ass to the courthouse. We hadn't even discussed it before, but now that she's said it out loud, I can't stop the visions of her with my rings around her finger and my name.

"Yeah…about that. It just kind of came out. I don't want you to freak out or anything about it. I understand that kind of step takes time."

"Says fucking who?" I interrupt.

"Uh…I don't know? Everyone?"

"Jesus, Em. I think it's safe to say we aren't just like everyone. Everything about the road we've had to travel to get to this point has been pretty off the tracks of normal. Who says we need to go in a certain order?" I place my hand against her stomach before continuing. "Pretty sure we proved that point over and over."

"Yeah," she laughs. "I guess we did."

"Just you wait, Emersyn Keeze. You're going to marry me as soon as we get home, and then I'm going to spend every day blessing you with everything I have."

"You're going to marry me? Don't you think you should actually ask?"

God, I love that sass.

"Keep it up, Em. I'm going to start adding up all that sass again."

Her eyes widen at my low growl before she laughs in my face. "I'm going to look forward to it, Mad."

"You do that, angel."

I take her lips in a slow, sweet, and intoxicating kiss. By the time I pull back, her eyes are glossy, her cheeks are red, and her lips are swollen. I lean forward, pull her plump bottom lip in my mouth, and nibble lightly, earning a moan from Emmy.

"Blessed," I whisper against her lips.

WE DIDN'T spend long in the hospital. After she was monitored overnight and her bleeding stopped with fluids, we were released with the referral to follow up with her home obstetrics physician. We got a prescription for the urinary tract infection she had, another factor that the doctor said had caused her bleeding. She needs to keep herself hydrated, and as long as everything looks good at her doctor appointment, he doesn't see us having any lasting issues.

We took our time getting home. Instead of flying, we kept our rental car and decided to make a two-week road trip out of our drive home, stopping in a different hotel each night and spending time together.

Axel called three days into our trip and said that there was some man named Jefferson calling the office nonstop. Judging by the fact that he yelled it over the line before hanging up, I'm guessing that Jefferson has been quite persistent. I figured it would happen, but I didn't think she would rally that quickly.

"Do you want me to sit with you when you call him back?" Emmy asks later that night when we check into our hotel somewhere in the middle of Mississippi.

"Yeah. It shouldn't take that long. He's most likely feeling me out and seeing just what I want out of that bitch."

"And? What do you want?"

"Honestly, Em…I'm not really sure. I don't want a part of Locke Oil. I don't even want their blood money. I just… I just want to be done with them. But then I think about everything they played a part in and all of the years of pain before more years of fear. When I think about all of that, I want to be done with it, but I also want to take their hurt and turn it into something good."

She smiles and sits in my lap. "I can understand that. I think we can figure something out, baby. I'm ready to support whatever decision you make." She's quiet for a second, lightly rubbing my chest with her hand. "I've been meaning to ask… How did you know about all that stuff anyway about them and the company? I never did get a chance to ask you."

Her hands start roaming my chest more freely, and for a second, I can't speak because I'm too busy telling my cock to calm the fuck down.

"When we decided that eventually we would be going out there, I started looking into everything I could. Some searches not so legal. Their downfall with the company wasn't hard to find. She spends more than she makes, according to her financial history. The fact that I still had my shares in the company was more shocking than anything. I guess, after everything that happened, I just wanted a clean break. I didn't want to touch anything that they could possibly hurt me more with. So when the random letter here or there came from Jefferson, their lawyer, or anything attached to them would hit my desk, I buried it."

She nods her head and then lays it on my shoulder, wrapping one of her arms behind my back. She continues to run her fingers against my chest while she thinks, and the whole time, I fight my body.

"So now that you know? Do you want to go through with your threat to take her for everything she has? Or do you want to talk about other options? I think I have an idea you might be open to."

I think about her question for a moment. I've been asking myself the same thing since we left the hospital. It's like running in a constant circle.

"I really don't think I want their money. Now especially. She's an evil bitch, Em. I don't want to do something out of spite and vengeance that has her coming after us later just because she thinks we're sitting on *her* pile of money or something. I think I'm going to have Jefferson draw something up that I sign them over with the stipulation that none of them can contact us again."

She doesn't say anything for so long that I wonder if she has fallen asleep.

"Can I suggest something else? You can do whatever you need, baby, and I'll support you one hundred and fifty perfect, but what about selling and donating your money? I know that you're struggling with what accepting this money means to all that you've overcome, but taking the money that is owed to you will not make you one of them, Maddox. I was looking into the Semper Fi Fund, and I think this might be a good charity for you to donate to. Your family played such a gigantic part in how you've lived your life for the last twelve years. Especially after your injury—when you needed them the most. What a better way to kind of help karma out than to take the money from the three people whom didn't support you when you needed them the most and give it to a charity that will help other fallen marines when they might not have anyone either?"

I'm intimately familiar with how important the Semper Fi Fund can be to an injured member of the military. I wouldn't have been able to pick up the shattered pieces of my life if it hadn't been for their funding, resources, and help in transitioning into my new life.

"God, I love you, Em. I didn't even think about that, but I think it's a great idea. I'll make sure that it's in the paperwork from Jefferson. Complete sale of my shares in Locke Oil and all money be donated to the Semper Fi Fund. But I'm making sure he also includes that they can't contact us or any of our children. I just want it done. I'm sick of the baby steps, Em… You told me once that we had to learn to walk again before we could run. Well, angel, it's time for us to run."

I feel her cheek move when she smiles.

"You're right, baby. I'm ready to run," she whispers.

# EPILOGUE
## Maddox

### Five Years Later

"STOP SQUIRMING, Emersyn," I rasp in her ear.

"Don't you give me that tone, Maddox Locke."

"Watch that sass, Emersyn Locke."

She narrows her eyes and then closes them tight. She's been making that same face for the last thirty minutes, and every time I tell her to stop wiggling that sexy ass around, she throws her sass back in my face. I can't wait to spank her ass later for it.

"Almost done," Rex says.

I look over her body and give him a nod.

"You said that ten minutes ago," she reminds him.

"Yeah. Then you started acting like a baby," he laughs at her, returning to his task.

"Watch it, Em."

Her eyes snap open again and I laugh. Oh, it's going to be a fun night.

Bending over so that my lips are against her ear, I promise, "You're lucky I got a babysitter for the whole night. By the time I finish, you're going to be knocking the frames off the walls with your screams."

"Ugh!"

I laugh again and she rolls her eyes.

"You two need to get all that shit out of your system before you come in here next time. Fuck, man. My girl's out of town for another week and I have my two horniest motherfucking clients in my chair again. Every damn time."

"Hey, watch your shit," I snap.

"Watch my shit? You're the one saying the shit. Not my fault my ears work." He looks down at Emmy, pulls his gloves off, and stands. "All done."

"Good. Now, get out."

"You can't tell me to get out, dude. I own the place."

"Just did, Rex. Give me a second with my wife."

He mumbles under his breath about annoying customers, but he leaves the room and shuts the door.

I lean down, and look at Emmy's naked torso, and smile.

Right on her ribs, sitting under her bra line, is a big-ass antique padlock. The center has a detailed keyhole, and the way Rex shaded her blacks with gray gives it an almost three-dimensional feel. The shackle is engaged with the lock, holding it closed, but along the curve in masculine scrawl is the one word that sets my blood on fire.

## Maddox

SEEING MY name permanently inked into her skin is the biggest turn-on.

The rest of the tattoo though… There are no words for how big my heart feels right now.

There are two hearts locked in. The first heart has our first daughter's name on it and the other with our second-born daughter's name.

Maddisyn was born four years ago and hasn't stopped screaming since. She has been my shadow since the day she learned to crawl. Wherever I went, she would follow. Her sister, Emberlyn, was born two years ago and is our silent thinker. She gave us one giant cry when she was born then settled in and let everyone fuss over her. She's been the same since day one.

We've been talking about having another baby for a few months now, and as much as I love seeing her pregnant, I'm not sure if I can handle another daughter. The first time Maddisyn told me that she had a boyfriend, I almost lost my shit. At least this way, with two, I can keep my eye on one and Emmy can help with the other.

"Damn, Em."

"Looks good, hmm?" she asks.

I help her off the table and she walks over to the mirror. With tears in her eyes and a smile on her face, she admires it. I can tell that she loves it.

"Looks perfect."

She turns and her eyes go to my chest—more specifically, my newest tattoo. Across my chest, with a slight curve, is the one word that has come to mean so much over the last five-plus years.

BLESSED

Emmy had the idea to add two sparrow birds on either side, one for each of our girls, and altogether, it makes the perfect tattoo to represent our life together.

"I love you," she sighs, not taking her eyes off my chest.

"I love you back," I reply.

"Let's get out of here so we can enjoy a night of you making me scream the walls down."

When I yell for Rex, he comes to finish cleaning and covering her new tattoo. I toss a few bills down, grab her hand, and drag her out of the tattoo shop.

Time to get my wife home and show her how much I love seeing my name on her body.

"I CAN'T take anymore, Mad! Please, baby!" she screams out in pleasure when I bring my hand down on her already pink ass.

I smooth the skin over with my palm before running my hand down to push two fingers deep inside her soaked pussy. Her walls try to hold my fingers in deep, and I know she's seconds away. If I give her a few deep thrusts, she is going to come hard.

But not yet.

"Please!"

"You can keep begging, Emersyn, but I'm not fucking this sweet cunt until I'm good and ready."

"I'm ready, you big jerk!" she yells over her shoulder.

I bring my hand down again and grab her firm flesh in a hard grip. "Watch that damn sass."

She wiggles again, her stomach moving against my swollen cock, causing me to groan.

I give her another smack just for making my cock even harder. Her skin is now bright with my handprints and her wetness is coating her thighs. I lean back and drop my body to the bed. I was sitting on the edge with her resting over my knees, but now, I need to eat her pussy until I've had my fill.

"Get up here and give me that pussy, Em."

She hurries off my lap and climbs up my chest, her wet center slick and hot against my body as she moves to straddle my face. I look up and meet her bright eyes before lifting my hands, grabbing her hips, and pushing her to my waiting mouth.

I feast on her delicious cunt. My tongue swirls around her swollen nub before I nibble on her smooth lips. She cries out when I suck her clit into my mouth with a hard suction. When I feel her juices soak my chin, I smile against her skin.

Then I smack her ass and give her one last lick.

"You want to ride my cock or do you want me to fuck you into the mattress?"

"I can't move my legs, baby," she sighs.

"Then get on your back, Emersyn."

After she moves off me, I stand next to the bed and wait until her legs are hanging off the edge. When she wants it hard and fast, this is the easiest position to give her that. She wraps those long legs around my waist and lets me drive my cock into her body.

"Next time, I want your mouth on my dick," I demand before pushing in slowly. "You want it hard, angel?"

"Yes, Maddox, please—fuck me hard."

I give her what she wants. My hips slam into hers, and just like I promised earlier, her cries echo off the walls all throughout our house.

# Emmy

"COME ON, Em! It's time to go get the girls!"

I finish pulling my shirt over my head, cringing a little when I brush over my tender side. I couldn't be happier with the way my lock turned out. When we talked about a way for me to get a tattoo like the rose he has for me, this was the first thing he came up with and it stuck.

I shove my feet into my shoes and rush down the stairs to where Maddox is spinning the keys to his truck. He didn't waste a second parting with his Charger when we found out that I was pregnant with Maddisyn. I miss it, but his big, black beast is pretty hot too.

"You act like I'm making us late. Need I remind you that I would have been ready an hour ago if you hadn't wanted to eat me instead of breakfast."

"You didn't complain when you had my cock down your throat, Emersyn, so don't act like it's my fault alone."

I grumble but walk past him. His hand comes down on my ass, and I turn to scowl at him.

"Sass," he states with a shrug, dips low, and gives me a hard kiss. "It's not any fun when I can't take my time with you, so next time, I'll wake you up a few hours earlier."

"Aren't you supposed to slow down with old age?"

He frowns and I laugh. He made me shave his head when his gray started coming in. I thought it was so hot, but he wanted it off. So the buzz cut is back. I miss having his thicker hair to run my fingers through, but when I feel that prickly sensation along my thighs when he has his tongue busy between my legs, it's pretty hot.

"You keep reminding me that I pushed over into my forties and I'm going to remind you that you need my baby in your belly before you hit your mid-thirties."

"Hey! I still have a couple of years to go!"

We laugh and continue our banter on the way to Axel and Izzy's house. They wanted to keep the girls last night for us to enjoy a date night. We had Nate and Dani the weekend before, so they owed us a good night out. Nate turned eight this year, so the co-ed sleepovers are starting to make Maddox go crazy. I keep reminding him that they're just kids, but it doesn't do any good.

We must be later than I thought because everyone is already here when we arrive. Melissa's minivan is parked half on the grass and her back doors are wide open. Those two have so many kids that it's no wonder they forget to close their doors every time we go somewhere. They had their second set of twins, boys this time, last year—Camden and Colton. I have no idea how Melissa is still standing, smiling, and full of energy with five children. Cohen is about to turn eleven and the twins, Lyn and Lila, are going to be seven soon.

Beck and Dee's car is behind theirs, her 'prince on board' sticker still hanging in the back window. They had their son, Liam, a few months before Maddisyn. They've been best friends ever since. They've tried for a while to have a second child, but it doesn't seem to be in the cards for them.

Asher's Jeep, which he refuses to get rid of even if Chelcie says the wheels are going to fall off any day now, is covered in mud. I bet Axel had a shit fit when he pulled up. They had their second child, Jaxon, four years ago. They didn't want to wait after Zac was born, choosing to keep their children close in age. They're almost the exact age difference that Asher and Coop were. Zac, sweet little Zac, is so much like his father was. He's so full of life—never wanting to sit out of the fun when he can be the center of it.

"Sway and Davey aren't coming?" I ask Maddox when we climb out of his truck.

"I thought they were, but I know they had Stella down at the lake this weekend, so they might have just stayed another day."

"How is Sway dealing with his daughter starting school this year?"

"He's stopped coming into the office to see Davey, so I guess better."

"That's good. I know he was having issues with their princess growing up," I laugh.

That would be a vast understatement. When Sway realized that the summer was almost over and Stella would be starting kindergarten in a few weeks, he called out of work for a week. When Davey finally got him to go back to work, he brought Stella with him. She was like a glitter-throwing fairy for hours. I went in to get my hair done and left with so much of it falling off my head that I think I'm still finding flecks in my car.

Sway and Davey had their commitment ceremony almost four

years ago, and after years of fighting for adopting their own child, they found Stella. The paperwork was finalized six months ago, and I swear I've never seen him happier.

I never did go back to work at Corps Security. Maddox and I both agreed that we wanted our children to grow up with one of us home. He started working shorter hours at the office, and when we bought our house, he set up his home office so that he could be able to do most of his work there.

Walking up the path to their home, we can hear all the children yelling over each other before we even open the door. I look up at my husband's carefree, smiling face. He gives me a wink, opens the door, and runs through when he sees Maddisyn laughing at him from the hallway. Her squeals and loud giggles trail behind her.

I watch his retreating form running at full speed after our daughter and smile. We've come so far. He was ready to run five years ago and we haven't stopped since.

## Maddox

"I DON'T like the way your son is looking at my daughter," Axel grumbles, crossing his arms over his chest and looking over at where Cohen and Dani are laughing by the docks.

"Seriously, Ax! He's ten. I think it's time for you to stop acting like a damn ape when your daughter is around anyone with a penis." Izzy slaps his arm and gives Greg a wink. "Plus, I think it's cute."

"Watch it, Izzy. It isn't cute. That's my baby girl you're talking about there."

"What are you going to do when she starts dating?" I ask, taking a deep pull from my beer.

"Like hell. She isn't fucking dating. Ever."

I laugh at him, taking another deep swallow.

"Laugh now. If she starts dating, I'm sure your girls won't be far behind her." He laughs when I spit my beer out.

Turning to meet his laughter, I frown and give him a hard glare. "Not fucking happening."

"Famous last words, brother," he says before raising his beer in toast. "To making sure that no dicks come near our daughters and that we never run out of ammo."

"Idiots," Izzy grumbles and walks towards their backyard, where all the kids are running around through the sprinklers they have set up. "Go get the grill started, Ax!" she calls over her shoulder and bends to grab a wobbling Colt, giving him a loud, wet raspberry against his stomach.

"Hard to believe how much life has changed since we got to Georgia," Beck says to my left.

"You aren't lying," Greg laughs, his eyes scanning the yard for his wife.

I follow his eyes to where our wives are all standing in a circle and laughing. Kids are randomly running into their circle for hugs and then back out just as quickly. When my eyes meet Emmy's from across the yard, she gives me a warm smile, which I return with one of my own.

God, I'm one lucky son of a bitch. I have a life so full of blessings that I don't even remember the dark days when, before, I never thought this was possible.

# FIFTEEN (PLUS A FEW) YEARS LATER

"DADDY!"

"Maddisyn," I call back, laughing when she comes running into my office so fast that she overshoots the door and runs into the wall. "Good God, girl. What has you running like the bats of hell are chasing you?"

She bends over, her long, black hair pulled high in a ponytail, and gasps for her breath.

"Daddy!" I hear being called farther through the house and roll my eyes. I should have known that Emberlyn wouldn't be far behind her sister if it's something they deem this important.

"Yup, Ember. Just follow your sister's loud-ass breathing or maybe look for the hole her head left in the wall."

"Not funny, Daddy," Maddi scolds.

"Hilarious, daughter."

"Whatevs." She plops down on the couch and crosses one of her long, bare legs over the other. I frown when I see how short her shorts are, something she doesn't miss. "Don't even start with me. I'm twenty years old, Daddy. It's time you stopped acting like a crazy person when you don't like what I wear."

"Like hell!" I boom, running my hand through my hair, now thick with growth and scattered with what Emmy calls a sexy salt-and-pepper look. Whatever the hell that means.

"Daddy!" Emberlyn gasps when she bursts into the office.

"Yes, Ember?"

Unlike her sister, she's dressed with actual clothes that cover her body. Her jeans might be too tight though. And I definitely don't like the top of her shirt coming down that far. I scowl at her, but she just waves me off.

"Did you hear? Dani has a date and Mom said that Uncle Ax is flipping his shit!"

"Don't say shit, Ember."

"Why the hell not? You do."

"Yeah, well, when you're as old as I am, I don't care what you fucking say," I rebuke.

"Whatevs. Did you even hear what I said?"

"I did, but I'm not sure what the big deal is. Dani is almost twenty-two. I'm thinking it's time for him to stop flipping the hell out."

"Does that mean you'll stop acting like a freak when I go out on dates?" Maddisyn laughs.

"I don't fucking think so."

"That's what I thought."

"So, please tell me what on Earth is so shocking about this big date that has you two running around like lunatics?"

"Oh, get ready for this," Emmy says from the doorway before walking in. I move my chair back and wait for her to sit. "Everyone is freaking out because little Dani Reid is going on a date with Cohen Cage."

Well, shit.

THE END

For more information on the Semper Fi Fund and how you can help, please visit:

www.SemperFiFund.org

# ACKNOWLEDGMENTS

This is probably one of the hardest books I've written to date. The closer that I got to the end I was silently sobbing knowing that I was about to say goodbye to one amazing family.

I can't thank you – my readers – enough for every single second of love and support that you have given the Corps Security family and me. These books started out as a dream and they've turned into something that even I can't believe is real. Thank you to every single reader, blogger, author and friend that has been along this ride with me. I truly am a blessed woman.

To my family, for putting up with me when I get into tunnel vision writing mode. For dealing with the mountains of laundry when I forget that we still need clean stuff. For my husband cooking every meal—er...scratch that, you would do that anyway since we don't want to die if I cook. I love you, my crazy party of 5.

My editor Mickey. I can honestly say I wouldn't be anywhere without you. I have no idea how I survived without your brilliance before and I hope I never find out.

To Brenda Wright for getting the 6th ebook formatting together. Every single book I've written I've had you and your incredible friendship along the way. I love you, woman!

Stacey Blake – I don't even know where to start. ☺ I sometimes pull my paperbacks out and just flip through the pages with a huge smile. One that you're responsible for. I can't thank you enough for knowing exactly what I want and giving me even more. You're paperbacks are something that make me cry happy tears.

Michael Stokes – I really can't thank you enough for being the man behind this cover image. When I found this picture, this man, I knew he had to be my Maddox Locke. You made the process so effortless and for that, I thank you. You've given me the honor of having three of your images as the 'faces' of my men and I can't wait to work with you more in the future.

Thank you to Andee and Hollie. I would still be looking at a blank screen if it hadn't been for you two and your constant help. Hibachi and parking lot porn! <3

Rochelle Paige. I have no words to express this thank you. You were there when I needed you the most. You kept me from jumping off the ledge more times than I can count. I will forever owe you!

To Brooke Cumberland. Thank you for answering every single question that I threw at you and not wanting to bash my head in. Your help in making Maddox the man he is will be forever appreciated.

To my betas…I know I drive you crazy, but you still love me. HAHA! Seriously, this has been one hell of a ride and I can't thank you enough for everything that you've done for me.

Sofie Hartley, my UK sister. This is when I put it in writing. You know…for that sexy Mr. Black. Locke.Is.Yours. I give him to you with the promise that Emmy doesn't mind too much. Take care of him, he's special. I bloody love you! Now…make me some crumpets!

And finally…to the most important ladies in my life and truly the bestest friends a bitch could ask for. My FBGM crew. Rochelle Paige, Ella Fox, Aurora Rose Reynolds, Tessa Teevan and Kristi Webster. There isn't one damn thing I can't come to you ladies with. The good, bad, and ugly. The hot, disgusting and soul-sucking crazy. The best damn support system ever. I don't ever want to find out what it's like without our special brand of awesome. Hey—I owe y'all a bracelet.